ANIMAL HEROES

ANIMAL HEROES

by ERNEST THOMPSON SETON

ILLUSTRATED BY THE AUTHOR

GROSSET & DUNLAP
Publishers New York

SPECIAL GROSSET & DUNLAP EDITION

1966

PRINTED IN THE UNITED STATES OF AMERICA
LIBRARY OF CONGRESS CATALOG CARD NUMBER: 66-16583

To the Reader

A HERO is an individual of unusual gifts and achievements. Whether it be man or animal, this definition applies; and it is the histories of such that appeal to the imagination and to the hearts of those who hear them.

In this volume every one of the stories, though more or less composite, is founded on the actual life of a veritable animal hero. The most composite is the White Reindeer. This story I wrote by Utrovand in Norway during the summer of 1900, while the Reindeer herds grazed in sight on the near uplands.

The Lynx is founded on some of my own early experiences in the backwoods.

It is less than ten years since the 'Jack Warhorse' won his hero-crown. Thousands of "Kaskadoans" will remember him, and by the name *Warhorse* his coursing exploits are recorded in several daily papers.

The least composite is Arnaux. It is so nearly historical that several who knew the bird have supplied additional items of information.

The nest of the destroying Peregrines, with its owners and their young, is now to be seen in the American Museum of Natural History of New York. The Museum authorities inform me that Pigeon badges with the following numbers were found in the nest: 9970–S, 1696, ⌐ 63, 77, J. F. 52, Ex. 705, 6–1894, C 20900. Perhaps some Pigeon-lover may learn from these lines the fate of one or other wonderful flier that has long been recorded "never returned."

Contents

ANIMAL HEROES

Slum Cat

Slum Cat

LIFE I

1

-E-A-T! M-e-a-t!" came shrilling down Scrimper's Alley. Surely the Pied Piper of Hamelin was there, for it seemed that all the Cats in the neighborhood were running toward the sound, though the Dogs, it must be confessed, looked scornfully indifferent.

"Meat! Meat!" and louder; then the center of attraction came in view—a rough, dirty little man with a push-cart; while straggling behind him were a score of Cats that joined in his cry with a sound nearly the same as his own. Every fifty yards, that is, as soon as a goodly throng of Cats was gathered, the push-cart stopped. The man with the magic voice took out of the box in his cart a skewer on which were pieces of strong-smelling boiled liver. With a long stick he pushed the pieces off. Each Cat seized on one, and wheeling, with a slight depression of the ears and a little tiger growl and glare, she rushed away with her prize to devour it in some safe retreat.

"Meat! Meat!" And still they came to get their portions.

All were well known to the meat-man. There was Castiglione's Tiger; this was Jones's Black; here was Pralitsky's "Torkershell," and this was Madame Danton's White; there sneaked Blenkinshoff's Maltee, and that climbing on the barrow was Sawyer's old Orange Billy, an impudent fraud that never had had any financial backing—all to be remembered and kept in account. This one's owner was sure pay, a dime a week; that one's doubtful. There was John Washee's Cat, that got only a small piece because John was in arrears. Then there was the saloon-keeper's collared and ribboned ratter, which got an extra lump because the 'barkeep' was liberal; and the roundsman's Cat, that brought no cash, but got unusual consideration because the meat-man did. But there were others. A black Cat with a white nose came rushing confidently with the rest, only to be repulsed savagely. Alas! Pussy did not understand. She had been a pensioner of the barrow for months. Why this unkind change? It was beyond her comprehension. But the meat-man knew. Her mistress had stopped payment. The meat-man kept no books but his memory, and it never was at fault.

Outside this patrician 'four hundred' about the barrow, were other Cats, keeping away from the push-cart because they were not on the list, the Social Register as it were, yet fascinated by the heavenly smell and the faint possibility of accidental good luck. Among these hangers-on was a thin gray Slummer, a homeless Cat that lived by her wits—slab-sided and not over-clean. One could see at a glance that she was doing her duty by a family in some out-of-the-way corner. She kept one eye on the barrow circle and the other on the possible Dogs. She saw a score of happy Cats slink off with their delicious 'daily' and their tiger-like air, but no opening

for her, till a big Tom of her own class sprang on a little pensioner with intent to rob. The victim dropped the meat to
defend herself against the enemy, and before the 'all-powerful'
could intervene, the gray Slummer saw her chance, seized the
prize, and was gone.

She went through the hole in Menzie's side door and over
the wall at the back, then sat down and devoured the lump
of liver, licked her chops, felt absolutely happy, and set out
by devious ways to the rubbish-yard, where, in the bottom
of an old cracker-box, her family was awaiting her. A plain-
tive mewing reached her ears. She went at speed and reached
the box to see a huge Black Tom-cat calmly destroying her
brood. He was twice as big as she, but she went at him with
all her strength, and he did as most animals will do when
caught wrong-doing, he turned and ran away. Only one was
left, a little thing like its mother, but of more pronounced
color—gray with black spots, and a white touch on nose, ears,
and tail-tip. There can be no question of the mother's grief
for a few days; but that wore off, and all her care was for the
survivor. That benevolence was as far as possible from the
motives of the murderous old Tom there can be no doubt;
but he proved a blessing in deep disguise, for both mother and
Kit were visibly bettered in a short time. The daily quest for
food continued. The meat-man rarely proved a success, but
the ash-cans were there, and if they did not afford a meat-
supply, at least they were sure to produce potato-skins that
could be used to allay the gripe of hunger for another day.

One night the mother Cat smelled a wonderful smell that
came from the East River at the end of the alley. A new smell
always needs investigating, and when it is attractive as well
as new, there is but one course open. It led Pussy to the docks

a block away, and then out on a wharf, away from any cover but the night. A sudden noise, a growl and a rush, were the first notice she had that she was cut off by her old enemy, the Wharf Dog. There was only one escape. She leaped from the wharf to the vessel from which the smell came. The Dog could not follow, so when the fish-boat sailed in the morning Pussy unwillingly went with her and was seen no more.

2

The Slum Kitten waited in vain for her mother. The morning came and went. She became very hungry. Toward evening a deep-laid instinct drove her forth to seek food. She slunk out of the old box, and feeling her way silently among the rubbish, she smelled everything that seemed eatable, but without finding food. At length she reached the wooden steps leading down into Jap Malee's bird-store underground. The door was open a little. She wandered into a world of rank and curious smells and a number of living things in cages all about her. A Negro was sitting idly on a box in a corner. He saw the little stranger enter and watched it curiously. It wandered past some Rabbits. They paid no heed. It came to a wide-barred cage in which was a Fox. The gentleman with the bushy tail was in a far corner. He crouched low; his eyes glowed. The Kitten wandered, sniffing, up to the bars, put its head in, sniffed again, then made toward the feed-pan, to be seized in a flash by the crouching Fox. It gave a frightened "mew," but a single shake cut that short and would have ended Kitty's nine lives at once, had not the Negro come to the rescue. He had no weapon and could not get into the cage, but he spat with such copious vigor in the Fox's face that he dropped the Kitten and returned to the corner, there to sit blinking his eyes in sullen fear.

The Negro pulled the Kitten out. The shake of the beast of prey seemed to have stunned the victim, really to have saved it much suffering. The Kitten seemed unharmed, but giddy. It tottered in a circle for a time, then slowly revived, and a few minutes later was purring in the Negro's lap, apparently none the worse, when Jap Malee, the bird-man, came home.

Jap was not an Oriental; he was a full-blooded Cockney, but his eyes were such little accidental slits aslant in his round, flat face, that his first name was forgotten in the highly descriptive title of "Jap." He was not especially unkind to the birds and beasts whose sales were supposed to furnish his living, but his eye was on the main chance; he knew what he wanted. He didn't want the Slum Kitten.

The Negro gave it all the food it could eat, then carried it to a distant block and dropped it in a neighboring iron-yard.

3

One full meal is as much as any one needs in two or three days, and under the influence of this stored-up heat and power, Kitty was very lively. She walked around the piled-up rubbish, cast curious glances on far-away Canary-birds in cages that hung from high windows; she peeped over fences, discovered a large Dog, got quietly down again, and presently finding a sheltered place in full sunlight, she lay down and slept for an hour. A slight 'sniff' awakened her, and before her stood a large Black Cat with glowing green eyes, and the thick neck and square jaws that distinguish the Tom; a scar marked his cheek, and his left ear was torn. His look was far from friendly; his ears moved backward a little, his tail twitched, and a faint, deep sound came from his throat. The Kitten innocently walked toward him. She did not remember him. He rubbed the sides of his jaws on a post, and quietly, slowly turned and disappeared. The last that she saw of him was the end of his tail twitching from side to side; and the little Slummer had no idea that she had been as near death to-day, as she had been when she ventured into the fox-cage.

As night came on the Kitten began to feel hungry. She examined carefully the long invisible colored stream that the wind is made of. She selected the most interesting of its strands, and, nose-led, followed. In the corner of the iron-yard was a box of garbage. Among this she found something that answered fairly well for food; a bucket of water under a faucet offered a chance to quench her thirst.

The night was spent chiefly in prowling about and learning the main lines of the iron-yard. The next day she passed as before, sleeping in the sun. Thus the time wore on. Sometimes she found a good meal at the garbage-box, sometimes there was nothing. Once she found the big Black Tom there, but discreetly withdrew before he saw her. The water-bucket was usually at its place, or, failing that, there were some muddy little pools on the stone below. But the garbage-box was very unreliable. Once it left her for three days without food. She searched along the high fence, and seeing a small hole, crawled through that and found herself in the open street. This was a new world, but before she had ventured

far, there was a noisy, rumbling rush—a large Dog came
bounding, and Kitty had barely time to run back into the
hole in the fence. She was dreadfully hungry, and glad to find
some old potato-peelings, which gave a little respite from
the hunger-pang. In the morning she did not sleep, but
prowled for food. Some Sparrows chirruped in the yard.
They were often there, but now they were viewed with new
eyes. The steady pressure of hunger had roused the wild
hunter in the Kitten; those Sparrows were game—were food.
She crouched instinctively and stalked from cover to cover, but
the chirpers were alert and flew in time. Not once, but many
times, she tried without result except to confirm the Sparrows in the list of things to be eaten if obtainable.

On the fifth day of ill luck the Slum Kitty ventured forth
into the street, desperately bent on finding food. When far
from the haven hole some small boys opened fire at her with
pieces of brick. She ran in fear. A Dog joined in the chase,
and Kitty's position grew perilous; but an old-fashioned iron
fence round a house-front was there, and she slipped in between the rails as the Dog overtook her. A woman in a window above shouted at the Dog. Then the boys dropped a
piece of cat-meat down to the unfortunate; and Kitty had the
most delicious meal of her life. The stoop afforded a refuge.
Under this she sat patiently till nightfall came with quiet,
then sneaked back like a shadow to her old iron-yard.

Thus the days went by for two months. She grew in size
and strength and in an intimate knowledge of the immediate
neighborhood. She made the acquaintance of Downey Street,
where long rows of ash-cans were to be seen every morning.
She formed her own ideas of their proprietors. The big house
was to her, not a Roman Catholic mission, but a place whose

garbage-tins abounded in choicest fish scrapings. She soon made the acquaintance of the meat-man, and joined in the shy fringe of Cats that formed the outer circle. She also met the Wharf Dog as well as two or three other horrors of the same class. She knew what to expect of them and how to avoid them; and she was happy in being the inventor of a new industry. Many thousand Cats have doubtless hung, in hope, about the tempting milk-cans that the early milk-man leaves on steps and window-ledges, and it was by the merest accident that Kitty found one with a broken lid, and so was taught to raise it and have a satisfying drink. Bottles, of course, were beyond her, but many a can has a misfit lid, and Kitty was very painstaking in her efforts to discover the loose-jointed ones. Finally she extended her range by exploration till she achieved the heart of the next block, and farther, till once more among the barrels and boxes of the yard behind the bird-man's cellar.

The old iron-yard never had been home, she had always felt like a stranger there; but here she had a sense of owner-ship, and at once resented the presence of another small Cat. She approached this newcomer with threatening air. The two had got as far as snarling and spitting when a bucket of water from an upper window drenched them both and effectually cooled their wrath. They fled, the newcomer over the wall, Slum Kitty under the very box where she had been born. This whole back region appealed to her strongly, and here again she took up her abode. The yard had no more garbage food than the other and no water at all, but it was frequented by stray Rats and a few Mice of the finest quality; these were occasionally secured, and afforded not only a palatable meal, but were the cause of her winning a friend.

4

Kitty was now fully grown. She was a striking-looking Cat of the tiger type. Her marks were black on a very pale gray, and the four beauty-spots of white on nose, ears, and tail-tip lent a certain distinction. She was very expert at getting a living, and yet she had some days of starvation and failed in her ambition of catching a Sparrow. She was quite alone, but a new force was coming into her life.

She was lying in the sun one August day, when a large Black Cat came walking along the top of a wall in her direction. She recognized him at once by his torn ear. She slunk into her box and hid. He picked his way gingerly, bounded lightly to a shed that was at the end of the yard, and was crossing the roof when a Yellow Cat rose up. The Black Tom glared and growled, so did the Yellow Tom. Their tails lashed from side to side. Strong throats growled and yowled. They approached each other with ears laid back, with muscles a-tense.

"Yow—yow—ow!" said the Black One.

"Wow—w—w!" was the slightly deeper answer.

"Ya—wow—wow—wow!" said the Black One, edging up half an inch nearer.

"Yow—w—w!" was the Yellow answer, as the blond Cat rose to full height and stepped with vast dignity a whole inch forward. "Yow—w!" and he went another inch, while his tail went swish, thump, from one side to the other.

"Ya—wow—yow—w!" screamed the Black in a rising tone, and he backed the eighth of an inch, as he marked the broad, unshrinking breast before him.

Windows opened all around, human voices were heard, but the Cat scene went on.

"Yow—yow—ow!" rumbled the Yellow Peril, his voice deepening as the other's rose. "Yow!" and he advanced another step.

Now their noses were but three inches apart; they stood sidewise, both ready to clinch, but each waiting for the other. They glared for three minutes in silence and like statues, except that each tail-tip was twisting.

The Yellow began again. "Yow—ow—ow!" in deep tone.

"Ya—a—a—a—a!" screamed the Black, with intent to strike terror by his yell; but he retreated one sixteenth of an inch. The Yellow walked up a long half-inch; their whiskers were mixing now; another advance, and their noses almost touched.

"Yo—w—w!" said Yellow, like a deep moan.

"Y—a—a—a—a—a—a!" screamed the Black, but he retreated a thirty-second of an inch, and the Yellow Warrior closed and clinched like a demon.

Oh, how they rolled and bit and tore, especially the Yellow One!

How they pitched and gripped and hugged, but especially the Yellow One!

Over and over, sometimes one on top, sometimes another, but mostly the Yellow One; and farther till they rolled off the roof, amid cheers from all the windows. They lost not a second in that fall to the junk-yard; they tore and clawed all the way down, but especially the Yellow One. And when they struck the ground, still fighting, the one on top was chiefly the Yellow One; and before they separated both had had as much as they wanted, especially the Black One! He scaled a wall and, bleeding and growling, disappeared, while the news was passed from window to window that Cayley's Black had been licked at last by Orange Billy.

Either the Yellow Cat was a very clever seeker, or else Slum Kitty did not hide very hard; but he discovered her among the boxes, and she made no attempt to get away, probably because she had witnessed the fight. There is nothing like success in warfare to win the female heart, and thereafter the Yellow Tom and Kitty became very good friends, not sharing each other's lives or food,—Cats do not do that way much,—but recognizing each other as entitled to special friendly privileges.

5

September had gone. October's shortening days were on when an event took place in the old cracker-box. If Orange Billy had come he would have seen five little Kittens curled up in the embrace of their mother, the little Slum Cat. It was a wonderful thing for her. She felt all the elation an animal mother can feel, all the delight, and she loved them and licked them with a tenderness that must have been a surprise to herself, had she had the power to think of such things.

She had added a joy to her joyless life, but she had also added a care and a heavy weight to her heavy load. All her strength was taken now to find food. The burden increased as the offspring grew up big enough to scramble about the boxes, which they did daily during her absence after they were six weeks old. That troubles go in flocks and luck in streaks, is well known in Slumland. Kitty had had three encounters with Dogs, and had been stoned by Malee's helper during a two days' starve. Then the tide turned. The very

next morning she found a full milk-can without a lid, successfully robbed a barrow pensioner, and found a big fish-
head, all within two hours. She had just returned with that
perfect peace which comes only of a full stomach, when she
saw a little brown creature in her junk-yard. Hunting memo-
ries came back in strength; she didn't know what it was, but
she had killed and eaten several Mice, and this was evidently
a big Mouse with bob-tail and large ears. Kitty stalked it with
elaborate but unnecessary caution; the little Rabbit simply
sat up and looked faintly amused. He did not try to run, and
Kitty sprang on him and bore him off. As she was not hungry, she carried him to the cracker-box and dropped him
among the Kittens. He was not much hurt. He got over his
fright, and since he could not get out of the box, he snuggled
among the Kittens, and when they began to take their evening
meal he very soon decided to join them. The old Cat was
puzzled. The hunter instinct had been dominant, but absence
of hunger had saved the Rabbit and given the maternal instinct a chance to appear. The result was that the Rabbit
became a member of the family, and was thenceforth guarded
and fed with the Kittens.

Two weeks went by. The Kittens romped much among
the boxes during their mother's absence. The Rabbit could
not get out of the box. Jap Malee, seeing the Kittens about
the back yard, told the Negro to shoot them. This he was
doing one morning with a .22 caliber rifle. He had shot one
after another and seen them drop from sight into the cran-
nies of the lumber-pile, when the old Cat came running
along the wall from the dock, carrying a small Wharf Rat.
He had been ready to shoot her, too, but the sight of that
Rat changed his plans: a rat-catching Cat was worthy to live.
It happened to be the very first one she had ever caught, but

it saved her life. She threaded the lumber-maze to the cracker-box and was probably puzzled to find that there were no Kittens to come at her call, and the Rabbit would not partake of the Rat. Pussy curled up to nurse the Rabbit, but she called from time to time to summon the Kittens. Guided by that call, the Negro crawled quietly to the place, and peering down into the cracker-box, saw, to his intense surprise, that it contained the old Cat, a live Rabbit, and a dead Rat.

The mother Cat laid back her ears and snarled. The Negro withdrew, but a minute later a board was dropped on the opening of the cracker-box, and the den with its tenants, dead and alive, was lifted into the bird-cellar.

"Say, boss, look a-hyar—hyar's where de little Rabbit got to wot we lost. Yo' sho t'ought Ah stoled him for de 'tater-bake."

Kitty and Bunny were carefully put in a large wire cage and exhibited as a happy family till a few days later, when the Rabbit took sick and died.

Pussy had never been happy in the cage. She had enough to eat and drink, but she craved her freedom—would likely have gotten 'death or liberty' now, but that during the four days' captivity she had so cleaned and slicked her fur that her unusual coloring was seen, and Jap decided to keep her.

LIFE II

6

Jap Malee was as disreputable a little Cockney bantam as ever sold cheap Canary-birds in a cellar. He was extremely poor, and the Negro lived with him because the 'Henglishman' was willing to share bed and board, and otherwise admit a perfect equality that few Americans conceded. Jap was perfectly honest according to his lights, but he hadn't any lights; and it was well known that his chief revenue was derived from storing and restoring stolen Dogs and Cats. The half-dozen Canaries were mere blinds. Yet Jap believed in himself. "Hi tell you, Sammy, me boy, you'll see me with 'orses of my own yet," he would say, when some trifling success inflated his dirty little chest. He was not without ambition, in a weak, flabby, once-in-a-while way, and he sometimes wished to be known as a fancier. Indeed, he had once gone to the wild length of offering a Cat for exhibition at the Knickerbocker High Society Cat and Pet Show, with three not overclear objects: first, to gratify his ambition; second, to secure the exhibitor's free pass; and, third, "well, you kneow, one 'as to kneow the valuable Cats, you kneow, when one goes a-catting." But this was a society show, the exhibitor had to be introduced, and his miserable alleged half-Persian was scornfully rejected.

The 'Lost and Found' columns of the papers were the only ones of interest to Jap, but he had noticed and saved a clipping about 'breeding for fur.' This was stuck on the wall of his den, and under its influence he set about what seemed a cruel experiment with the Slum Cat. First, he soaked her dirty fur with stuff to kill the two or three kinds of creepers she wore; and, when it had done its work, he washed her thoroughly in soap and warm water, in spite of her teeth, claws, and yowls. Kitty was savagely indignant, but a warm and happy glow spread over her as she dried off in a cage near the stove, and her fur began to fluff out with wonderful softness and whiteness. Jap and his assistant were much pleased with the result, and Kitty ought to have been. But this was preparatory: now for the experiment. "Nothing is so good for growing fur as plenty of oily food and continued exposure to cold weather," said the clipping. Winter was at hand, and Jap Malee put Kitty's cage out in the yard, protected only from the rain and the direct wind, and fed her with all the oil-cake and fish-heads she could eat. In a week a change began to show. She was rapidly getting fat and sleek—she had nothing to do but get fat and dress her fur. Her cage was kept clean, and nature responded to the chill weather and the oily food by making Kitty's coat thicker and glossier every day, so that by midwinter she was an unusually beautiful Cat in the fullest and finest of fur, with markings that were at least a rarity. Jap was much pleased with the result of the experiment, and as a very little success had a wonderful effect on him, he began to dream of the paths of glory. Why not send the Slum Cat to the show now coming on? The failure of the year before made him more careful of details. " 'T won't do, ye kneow, Sammy, to henter 'er as a tramp Cat, ye kneow," he observed to his help; "but it kin be arranged to suit the Knickerbockers. Nothink like a good noime, ye kneow. Ye see now it had orter be 'Royal' somethink or other—nothink goes with the Knickerbockers like 'Royal' anythink. Now 'Royal Dick,' or 'Royal Sam,' 'ow's that? But 'owld on; them's Tom names. Oi say, Sammy, wot's the noime of that island where ye wuz born?"

"Analostan Island, sah, was my native vicinity, sah."

"Oi say, now, that's good, ye kneow. 'Royal Analostan,' by Jove! The onliest pedigreed 'Royal Analostan' in the 'ole sheow, ye kneow. Ain't that foine?" and they mingled their cackles.

"But we'll 'ave to 'ave a pedigree, ye kneow." So a very long fake pedigree on the recognized lines was prepared. One dark afternoon Sam, in a borrowed silk hat, delivered the Cat and the pedigree at the show door. The Negro did the honors. He had been a Sixth Avenue barber, and he could put on more pomp and lofty hauteur in five minutes than Jap Malee could have displayed in a lifetime, and this, doubtless, was one reason for the respectful reception awarded the Royal Analostan at the Cat Show.

Jap was very proud to be an exhibitor; but he had all a Cockney's reverence for the upper class, and when on the opening day he went to the door, he was overpowered to see the array of carriages and silk hats. The gateman looked at him sharply, but passed him on his ticket, doubtless taking him for stable-boy to some exhibitor. The hall had velvet carpets before the long row of cages. Jap, in his small cunning, was sneaking down the side rows, glancing at the Cats of all kinds, noting the blue ribbons and the reds, peering about but not daring to ask for his own exhibit, inly trembling to think what the gorgeous gathering of fashion would say if they discovered the trick he was playing on them. He had passed all around the outer aisles and seen many prize-winners, but no sign of Slum Kitty. The inner aisles were more crowded. He picked his way down them, but still no Kitty, and he decided that it was a mistake; the judges had rejected the Cat later. Never mind; he had his exhibitor's ticket, and now knew where several valuable Persians and Angoras were to be found.

In the middle of the centre aisle were the high-class Cats. A great throng was there. The passage was roped, and two policemen were in place to keep the crowd moving. Jap wrig-

gled in among them; he was too short to see over, and though
the richly gowned folks shrunk from his shabby old clothes,
he could not get near; but he gathered from the remarks
that the gem of the show was there.

"Oh, isn't she a beauty!" said one tall woman.

"What distinction!" was the reply.

"One cannot mistake the air that comes only from ages
of the most refined surroundings."

"How I should like to own that superb creature!"

"Such dignity—such repose!"

"She has an authentic pedigree nearly back to the Pharaohs,
I hear"; and poor, dirty little Jap marvelled at his own cheek
in sending his Slum Cat into such company.

"Excuse me, madame." The director of the show now appeared, edging his way through the crowd. "The artist of the
'Sporting Element' is here, under orders to sketch the 'pearl
of the show' for immediate use. May I ask you to stand a little
aside? That's it; thank you."

"Oh, Mr. Director, cannot you persuade him to sell that
beautiful creature?"

"Hm, I don't know," was the reply. "I understand he is a
man of ample means and not at all approachable; but I'll try,
I'll try, madame. He was quite unwilling to exhibit his treasure at all, so I understand from his butler. Here, you, keep
out of the way," growled the director, as the shabby little man
eagerly pushed between the artist and the blue-blooded Cat.
But the disreputable one wanted to know where valuable Cats
were to be found. He came near enough to get a glimpse of
the cage, and there read a placard which announced that "The
blue ribbon and *gold medal* of the Knickerbocker High Society Cat and Pet Show" had been awarded to the "thorough-

bred, pedigreed Royal Analostan, imported and exhibited by J. Malee, Esq., the well-known fancier. (Not for sale.)" Jap caught his breath and stared again. Yes, surely; there, high in a gilded cage, on velvet cushions, with four policemen for guards, her fur bright black and pale gray, her bluish eyes slightly closed, was his Slum Kitty, looking the picture of a Cat bored to death with a lot of fuss that she likes as little as she understands it.

7

Jap Malee lingered around that cage, taking in the remarks, for hours—drinking a draught of glory such as he had never known in life before and rarely glimpsed in his dreams. But he saw that it would be wise for him to remain unknown; his "butler" must do all the business.

It was Slum Kitty who made that show a success. Each day her value went up in her owner's eyes. He did not know what prices had been given for Cats, and thought that he was touching a record pitch when his "butler" gave the director authority to sell the Analostan for one hundred dollars.

This is how it came about that the Slum Cat found herself transferred from the show to a Fifth Avenue mansion. She evinced a most unaccountable wildness at first. Her objection to petting, however, was explained on the ground of her aristocratic dislike of familiarity. Her retreat from the Lap-dog onto the centre of the dinner-table was understood to express a deep-rooted though mistaken idea of avoiding a defiling touch. Her assaults on a pet Canary were condoned for the reason that in her native Orient she had been used to despotic

example. The patrician way in which she would get the cover
off a milk-can was especially applauded. Her dislike of her
silk-lined basket, and her frequent dashes against the plate-
glass windows, were easily understood: the basket was too
plain, and plate-glass was not used in her royal home. Her
spotting of the carpet evidenced her Eastern modes of thought.
The failure of her several attempts to catch Sparrows in the
high-walled back yard was new proof of the royal impotency
of her bringing up; while her frequent wallowings in the garbage-can were understood to be the manifestation of a little
pardonable high-born eccentricity. She was fed and pampered,
shown and praised; but she was not happy. Kitty was home-
sick! She clawed at that blue ribbon round her neck till she
got it off; she jumped against the plate-glass because that
seemed the road to outside; she avoided people and Dogs because they had always proved hostile and cruel; and she would
sit and gaze on the roofs and back yards at the other side of the
window, wishing she could be among them for a change.

But she was strictly watched, was never allowed outside—
so that all the happy garbage-can moments occurred while
these receptacles of joy were indoors. One night in March,
however, as they were set out a-row for the early scavenger, the
Royal Analostan saw her chance, slipped out of the door, and
was lost to view.

Of course there was a grand stir; but Pussy neither knew
nor cared anything about that—her one thought was to go
home. It may have been chance that took her back in the direction of Gramercy Grange Hill, but she did arrive there after
sundry small adventures. And now what? She was not at home,
and she had cut off her living. She was beginning to be hungry, and yet she had a peculiar sense of happiness. She

cowered in a front garden for some time. A raw east wind
had been rising, and now it came to her with a particularly
friendy message; man would have called it an unpleasant
smell of the docks, but to Pussy it was welcome tidings from
home. She trotted down the long street due east, threading the
rails of front gardens, stopping like a statue for an instant, or
crossing the street in search of the darkest side, and came at
length to the docks and to the water. But the place was strange.
She could go north or south. Something turned her southward; and, dodging among docks and Dogs, carts and Cats,
crooked arms of the bay and straight board fences, she got, in
an hour or two, among familiar scenes and smells; and, before the sun came up, she had crawled back weary and foot-
sore through the same old hole in the same old fence and over
a wall to her junk-yard back of the bird-cellar—yes, back into
the very cracker-box where she was born.

Oh, if the Fifth Avenue family could only have seen her in
her native Orient!

After a long rest she came quietly down from the cracker-
box toward the steps leading to the cellar, engaged in her old-
time pursuit of seeking for eatables. The door opened, and
there stood the Negro. He shouted to the bird-man inside:

"Say, boss, come hyar. Ef dere ain't dat dar Royal Ankalostan am comed back!"

Jap came in time to see the Cat jumping the wall. They
called loudly and in the most seductive, wheedling tones:
"Pussy, Pussy, poor Pussy! Come, Pussy!" But Pussy was not
prepossessed in their favor, and disappeared to forage in her
old-time haunts.

The Royal Analostan had been a windfall for Jap—had
been the means of adding many comforts to the cellar and
several prisoners to the cages. It was now of the utmost im-

portance to recapture her majesty. Stale meat-offal and other infallible lures were put out till Pussy, urged by the reëstablished hunger-pinch, crept up to a large fish-head in a box-trap; the Negro, in watching, pulled the string that dropped the lid, and, a minute later, the Analostan was once more among the prisoners in the cellar. Meanwhile Jap had been watching the 'Lost and Found' column. There it was, "$25 reward," etc. That night Mr. Malee's butler called at the Fifth Avenue mansion with the missing cat. "Mr. Malee's compliments, sah. De Royal Analostan had recurred in her recent proprietor's vicinity and residence, sah. Mr. Malee had pleasure in recuperating the Royal Analostan, sah." Of course Mr. Malee could not be rewarded, but the butler was open to any offer, and plainly showed that he expected the promised reward and something more.

Kitty was guarded very carefully after that; but so far from being disgusted with the old life of starving, and glad of her ease, she became wilder and more dissatisfied.

8

The spring was doing its New York best. The dirty little English Sparrows were tumbling over each other in their gutter brawls, Cats yowled all night in the areas, and the Fifth Avenue family were thinking of their country residence. They packed up, closed house, and moved off to their summer home, some fifty miles away, and Pussy, in a basket, went with them.

"Just what she needed: a change of air and scene to wean her away from her former owners and make her happy."

The basket was lifted into a Rumble-shaker. New sounds

and passing smells were entered and left. A turn in the course
was made. Then a roaring of many feet, more swinging of the
basket; a short pause, another change of direction, then some
clicks, some bangs, a long shrill whistle, and door-bells of a
very big front door; a rumbling, a whizzing, an unpleasant
smell, a hideous smell, a growing horrible, hateful choking
smell, a deadly, griping, poisonous stench, with roaring that
drowned poor Kitty's yowls, and just as it neared the point
where endurance ceased, there was relief. She heard clicks and
clacks. There was light; there was air. Then a man's voice
called, "All out for 125th Street," though of course to Kitty it
was a mere human bellow. The roaring almost ceased—did
cease. Later the rackety-bang was renewed with plenty of
sounds and shakes, though not the poisonous gas; a long, hollow, booming roar with a pleasant dock smell was quickly
passed, and then there was a succession of jolts, roars, jars,
stops, clicks, clacks, smells, jumps, shakes, more smells, more
shakes,—big shakes, little shakes,—gases, smokes, screeches,
doorbells, tremblings, roars, thunders, and some new smells,
raps, heavings, rumblings, and more smells, but all without
any of the feel that the direction is changed. When at last it
stopped, the sun came twinkling through the basket-lid. The
Royal Cat was lifted into a Rumble-shaker of the old familiar
style, and, swerving aside from their past course, very soon the
noises of its wheels were grittings and rattlings; a new and horrible sound was added—the barking of Dogs, big and little and
dreadfully close. The basket was lifted, and Slum Kitty had
reached her country home.

Every one was officiously kind. They wanted to please the
Royal Cat, but somehow none of them did, except, possibly,
the big, fat cook that Kitty discovered on wandering into the
kitchen. This unctuous person smelt more like a slum than

anything she had met for months, and the Royal Analostan was proportionately attracted. The cook, when she learned that fears were entertained about the Cat staying, said: "Shure, she'd 'tind to thot; wanst a Cat licks her futs, shure she's at home." So she deftly caught the unapproachable royalty in her apron, and committed the horrible sacrilege of greasing the soles of her feet with pot-grease. Of course Kitty resented it— she resented everything in the place; but on being set down she began to dress her paws and found evident satisfaction in that grease. She licked all four feet for an hour, and the cook triumphantly announced that now "shure she'd be apt to shtay." And stay she did, but she showed a most surprising and disgusting preference for the kitchen, the cook, and the garbage pail.

The family, though distressed by these distinguished peculiarities, were glad to see the Royal Analostan more contented and approachable. They gave her more liberty after a week or two. They guarded her from every menace. The Dogs were taught to respect her. No man or boy about the place would have dreamed of throwing a stone at the famous pedigreed Cat. She had all the food she wanted, but still she was not happy. She was hankering for many things, she scarcely knew what. She had everything—yes, but she wanted something else. Plenty to eat and drink—yes, but milk does not taste the same when you can go and drink all you want from a saucer; it has to be stolen out of a tin pail when you are belly-pinched with hunger and thirst, or it does not have the tang—it isn't milk.

Yes, there *was* a junk-yard back of the house and beside it and around it too, a big one, but it was everywhere poisoned and polluted with roses. The very Horses and Dogs had the wrong smells; the whole country round was a repellent desert of lifeless, disgusting gardens and hay-fields, without a single tenement or smoke-stack in sight. How she did hate it all! There was only one sweet-smelling shrub in the whole horrible place, and that was in a neglected corner. She did enjoy nipping that and rolling in the leaves; it was a bright spot in the grounds; but the only one, for she had not found a rotten fish-head nor seen a genuine garbage-can since she came, and altogether it was the most unlovely, unattractive, unsmellable spot she had ever known. She would surely have gone that first night had she had the liberty. The liberty was weeks in coming, and, meanwhile, her affinity with the cook had developed as a bond to keep her; but one day after a summer of discontent a succession of things happened to stir anew the slum instinct of the royal prisoner.

A great bundle of stuff from the docks had reached the country mansion. What it contained was of little moment, but it was rich with a score of the most piquant and winsome of dock and slum smells. The chords of memory surely dwell in the nose, and Pussy's past was conjured up with dangerous force. Next day the cook 'left' through some trouble over this very bundle. It was the cutting of cables, and that evening the youngest boy of the house, a horrid little American with no proper appreciation of royalty, was tying a tin to the blue-blooded one's tail, doubtless in furtherance of some altruistic project, when Pussy resented the liberty with a paw that wore five big fish-hooks for the occasion. The howl of downtrodden America roused America's mother. The deft and womanly blow that she aimed with her book was miraculously avoided, and Pussy took flight, up-stairs, of course. A hunted Rat runs down-stairs, a hunted Dog goes on the level, a hunted Cat runs up. She hid in the garret, baffled discovery, and waited till night came. Then, gliding down-stairs, she tried each screen-door in turn, till she found one unlatched, and escaped into the black August night. Pitch-black to man's eyes, it was simply gray to her, and she glided through the disgusting shrubbery and flower-beds, took a final nip at that one little bush that had been an attractive spot in the garden, and boldly took her back track of the spring.

How could she take a back track that she never saw? There is in all animals some sense of direction. It is very low in man and very high in Horses, but Cats have a large gift, and this mysterious guide took her westward, not clearly and definitely, but with a general impulse that was made definite simply because the road was easy to travel. In an hour she had covered two miles and reached the Hudson River. Her nose had told her many times that the course was true. Smell after smell came back, just as a man after walking a mile in a strange street may not recall a single feature, but will remember, on seeing it again, "Why, yes, I saw that before." So Kitty's main guide was the sense of direction, but it was her nose that kept reassuring her, "Yes, now you are right—we passed this place last spring."

At the river was the railroad. She could not go on the water; she must go north or south. This was a case where her sense of direction was clear; it said, "Go south," and Kitty trotted down the foot-path between the iron rails and the fence.

LIFE III

9

Cats can go very fast up a tree or over a wall, but when it comes to the long steady trot that reels off mile after mile, hour after hour, it is not the cat-hop, but the dog-trot, that counts. Although the travelling was good and the path direct, an hour had gone before two more miles were put between her and the Hades of roses. She was tired and a little foot-sore. She was thinking of rest when a Dog came running to the fence near by, and broke out into such a horrible barking close to her ear that Pussy leaped in terror. She ran as hard as she could down the path, at the same time watching to see if the Dog should succeed in passing the fence. No, not yet! but he ran close by it, growling horribly, while Pussy skipped along on the safe side. The barking of the Dog grew into a low rumble—a louder rumble and roaring—a terrifying thunder. A light shone. Kitty glanced back to see, not the Dog, but a huge Black Thing with a blazing red eye coming on, yowling and spitting like a yard full of Cats. She put forth all her powers to run, made such time as she had never made before, but dared not leap the fence. She was running like a Dog, was flying, but all in vain; the monstrous pursuer overtook her, but missed her in the darkness, and hurried past to be lost in the night, while Kitty crouched gasping for breath, half a mile nearer home since that Dog began to bark.

This was her first encounter with the strange monster, strange to her eyes only; her nose seemed to know him and told her this was another landmark on the home trail. But Pussy lost much of her fear of his kind. She learned that they were very stupid and could not find her if she slipped quietly under a fence and lay still. Before morning she had encountered several of them, but escaped unharmed from all.

About sunrise she reached a nice little slum on her home trail, and was lucky enough to find several unsterilized eatables in an ash-heap. She spent the day around a stable where

were two Dogs and a number of small boys, that between
them came near ending her career. It was so very like home;
but she had no idea of staying there. She was driven by the
old craving, and next evening set out as before. She had seen
the one-eyed Thunder-rollers all day going by, and was getting used to them, so travelled steadily all that night. The
next day was spent in a barn where she caught a Mouse, and
the next night was like the last, except that a Dog she encountered drove her backward on her trail for a long way. Several
times she was misled by angling roads, and wandered far
astray, but in time she wandered back again to her general
southward course. The days were passed in skulking under
barns and hiding from Dogs and small boys, and the nights
in limping along the track, for she was getting foot-sore; but
on she went, mile after mile, southward, ever southward—
Dogs, boys, Roarers, hunger—Dogs, boys, Roarers, hunger—
yet on and onward still she went, and her nose from time to
time cheered her by confidently reporting, "There surely is
a smell we passed last spring."

10

So a week went by, and Pussy, dirty, ribbonless, foot-sore,
and weary, arrived at the Harlem Bridge. Though it was en-
veloped in delicious smells, she did not like the look of that
bridge. For half the night she wandered up and down the
shore without discovering any other means of going south,
excepting some other bridges, or anything of interest except
that here the men were as dangerous as the boys. Somehow
she had to come back to it; not only its smells were familiar,

but from time to time, when a One-eye ran over it, there was that peculiar rumbling roar that was a sensation in the spring-time trip. The calm of the late night was abroad when she leaped to the timber stringer and glided out over the water. She had got less than a third of the way across when a thundering One-eye came roaring at her from the opposite end. She was much frightened, but knowing their stupidity and blindness, she dropped to a low side beam and there crouched in hiding. Of course the stupid Monster missed her and passed on, and all would have been well, but it turned back, or another just like it came suddenly spitting behind her. Pussy leaped to the long track and made for the home shore. She might have got there had not a third of the Red-eyed Terrors come screeching at her from that side. She was running her hardest, but was caught between two foes. There was nothing for it but a desperate leap from the timbers into—she didn't know what. Down, down, down—plop, splash, plunge into the deep water, not cold, for it was August, but oh, so horrible! She spluttered and coughed when she came to the top, glanced around to see if the Monsters were swimming after her, and struck out for shore. She had never learned to swim, and yet she swam, for the simple reason that a Cat's position and actions in swimming are the same as her position and actions in walking. She had fallen into a place she did not like; naturally she tried to *walk* out, and the result was that she swam ashore. Which shore? The home-love never fails: the south side was the only shore for her, the one nearest home. She scrambled out all dripping wet, up the muddy bank and through coal-piles and dust-heaps, looking as black, dirty, and unroyal as it was possible for a Cat to look.

Once the shock was over, the Royal-pedigreed Slummer began to feel better for the plunge. A genial glow without from the bath, a genial sense of triumph within, for had she not outwitted three of the big Terrors?

Her nose, her memory, and her instinct of direction inclined her to get on the track again; but the place was infested with those Thunder-rollers, and prudence led her to turn aside and follow the river-bank with its musky home-reminders; and thus she was spared the unspeakable horrors of the tunnel.

She was over three days learning the manifold dangers and complexities of the East River docks. Once she got by mistake on a ferryboat and was carried over to Long Island; but she took an early boat back. At length on the third night she reached familiar ground, the place she had passed the night of her first escape. From that her course was sure and rapid. She knew just where she was going and how to get there. She knew even the more prominent features in the Dog-scape now. She went faster, felt happier. In a little while surely she would be curled up in her native Orient—the old junk-yard. Another turn, and the block was in sight.

But—what! It was gone! Kitty couldn't believe her eyes; but she must, for the sun was not yet up. There where once had stood or leaned or slouched or straggled the houses of the block, was a great broken wilderness of stone, lumber, and holes in the ground.

Kitty walked all around it. She knew by the bearings and by the local color of the pavement that she was in her home, that there had lived the bird-man, and there was the old junk-yard; but all were gone, completely gone, taking their familiar odors with them, and Pussy turned sick at heart in the utter hopelessness of the case. Her place-love was her master-mood.

She had given up all to come to a home that no longer existed, and for once her sturdy little heart was cast down. She wandered over the silent heaps of rubbish and found neither consolation nor eatables. The ruin had taken in several of the blocks and reached back from the water. It was not a fire; Kitty had seen one of those things. This looked more like the work of a flock of the Red-eyed Monsters. Pussy knew nothing of the great bridge that was to rise from this very spot.

When the sun came up she sought for cover. An adjoining block still stood with little change, and the Royal Analostan retired to that. She knew some of its trails; but once there, was unpleasantly surprised to find the place swarming with Cats that, like herself, were driven from their old grounds, and when the garbage-cans came out there were several Slummers at each. It meant a famine in the land, and Pussy, after standing it a few days, was reduced to seeking her other home on Fifth Avenue. She got there to find it shut up and deserted. She waited about for a day; had an unpleasant experience with a big man in a blue coat, and next night returned to the crowded slum.

September and October wore away. Many of the Cats died of starvation or were too weak to escape their natural enemies. But Kitty, young and strong, still lived.

Great changes had come over the ruined blocks. Though silent on the night when she first saw them, they were crowded with noisy workmen all day. A tall building, well advanced on her arrival, was completed at the end of October, and Slum Kitty, driven by hunger, went sneaking up to a pail that a Negro had set outside. The pail, unfortunately, was not for garbage; it was a new thing in that region: a scrubbing-pail. A sad disappointment, but it had a sense of comfort—there were traces of a familiar touch on the handle. While she was studying it, the Negro elevator-boy came out again. In spite of his blue clothes, his odorous person confirmed the good impression of the handle. Kitty had retreated across the street. He gazed at her.

"Sho ef dat don't look like de Royal Ankalostan! Hyar, Pussy, Pussy, Pu-s-s-s-s-y! Co-o-o-o-m-e, Pu-u-s-s-sy, hyar! I 'spec's she's sho hungry."

Hungry! She hadn't had a real meal for months. The Negro went into the building and reappeared with a portion of his own lunch.

"Hyar, Pussy, Puss, Puss, Puss!" It seemed very good, but Pussy had her doubts of the man. At length he laid the meat on the pavement, and went back to the door. Slum Kitty came forward very warily; sniffed at the meat, seized it, and fled like a little Tigress to eat her prize in peace.

LIFE IV

11

This was the beginning of a new era. Pussy came to the door of the building now whenever pinched by hunger, and the good feeling for the Negro grew. She had never understood that man before. He had always seemed hostile. Now he was her friend, the only one she had.

One week she had a streak of luck. Seven good meals on seven successive days; and right on the top of the last meal she found a juicy dead Rat, the genuine thing, a perfect windfall. She had never killed a full-grown Rat in all her lives, but seized the prize and ran off to hide it for future use. She was crossing the street in front of the new building when an old enemy appeared,—the Wharf Dog,—and Kitty retreated, naturally enough, to the door where she had a friend. Just as she neared it, he opened the door for a well-dressed man to come out, and both saw the Cat with her prize.

"Hello! Look at that for a Cat!"

"Yes, sah," answered the Negro. "Dat's ma Cat, sah; she's a terror on Rats, sah! hez 'em about cleaned up, sah; dat's why she's so thin."

"Well, don't let her starve," said the man with the air of the landlord. "Can't you feed her?"

"De liver meat-man comes reg'lar, sah; quatah dollar a week, sah,' said Sammy, fully realizing that he was entitled to the extra fifteen cents for "the idea."

"That's all right. I'll stand it."

12

"M-e-a-t! M-e-a-t!" is heard the magnetic, cat-conjuring cry of the old liver-man, as his barrow is pushed up the glorified Scrimper's Alley, and Cats come crowding, as of yore, to receive their due.

There are Cats black, white, yellow, and gray to be remembered, and, above all, there are owners to be remembered. As the barrow rounds the corner near the new building it makes a newly scheduled stop.

"Hyar, you, get out o' the road, you common trash," cries the liver-man, and he waves his wand to make way for the little gray Cat with blue eyes and white nose. She receives an unusually large portion, for Sam is wisely dividing the returns evenly; and Slum Kitty retreats with her 'daily' into shelter of the great building, to which she is regularly attached. She has entered into her fourth life with prospects of happiness never before dreamed of. Everything was against her at first; now everything seems to be coming her way. It is very doubtful that her mind was broadened by travel, but she knew what she wanted and she got it. She has achieved her long-time great ambition by catching, not *a* Sparrow, but two of them, while they were clinched in mortal combat in the gutter.

There is no reason to suppose that she ever caught another Rat; but the Negro secures a dead one when he can, for purposes of exhibition, lest her pension be imperilled. The dead one is left in the hall till the proprietor comes; then it is apologetically swept away. "Well, drat Cat, sah; dat Royal Ankalostan blood, sah, is terrors on Rats."

She has had several broods since. Sam thinks the Yellow Tom is the father of some of them, and no doubt he is right.

He has sold her a number of times with a perfectly clear conscience, knowing quite well that it is only a question of a few days before the Royal Analostan comes back again. Doubtless he is saving the money for some honorable ambition. She has learned to tolerate the elevator, and even to ride up and down on it. The Negro stoutly maintains that once, when she heard the meat-man, while she was on the top floor, she managed to press the button that called the elevator to take her down.

She is sleek and beautiful again. She is not only one of the four hundred that form the inner circle about the liver-barrow, but she is recognized as the star pensioner among them.

The liver-man is positively respectful. Not even the cream-and-chicken fed Cat of the pawn-broker's wife has such a position as the Royal Analostan. But in spite of her prosperity, her social position, her royal name and fake pedigree, the greatest pleasure of her life is to slip out and go a-slumming in the gloaming, for now, as in her previous lives, she is at heart, and likely to be, nothing but a dirty little Slum Cat.

Arnaux

THE CHRONICLE OF A HOMING PIGEON

Arnaux

1

W E passed through the side door of a big stable on West Nineteenth Street. The mild smell of the well-kept stalls was lost in the sweet odor of hay, as we mounted a ladder and entered the long garret. The south end was walled off, and the familiar "Coo-oo, cooooo-oo, ruk-at-a-coo," varied with the "whirr, whirr, whirr" of wings, informed us that we were at the pigeon-loft.

This was the home of a famous lot of birds, and to-day there was to be a race among fifty of the youngsters. The owner of the loft had asked me, as an unprejudiced outsider, to be judge in the contest.

It was a training race of the young birds. They had been taken out for short distances with their parents once or twice, then set free to return to the loft. Now for the first time they were to be flown without the old ones. The point of start, Elizabeth, N. J., was a long journey for their first unaided attempt. "But then," the trainer remarked, "that's how we weed out the fools; only the best birds make it, and that's all we want back."

There was another side to the flight. It was to be a race among those that did return. Each of the men about the loft as well as several neighboring fanciers were interested in one or other of the Homers. They made up a purse for the winner, and on me was to devolve the important duty of deciding which should take the stakes. Not the first bird *back,* but the first bird *into the loft,* was to win, for one that returns to his neighborhood merely, without immediately reporting at home, is of little use as a letter-carrier.

The Homing Pigeon used to be called the Carrier because it carried messages, but here I found that name restricted to the show bird, the creature with absurdly developed wattles; the one that carries the messages is now called the Homer, or Homing Pigeon—the bird that always comes home. These Pigeons are not of any special color, nor have they any of the fancy adornments of the kind that figure in Bird shows. They are not bred for style, but for speed and for their mental gifts. They must be true to their home, able to return to it without fail. The sense of direction is now believed to be located in the bony labyrinth of the ear. There is no creature with finer sense of locality and direction than a good Homer, and the only visible proofs of it are the great bulge on each side of the head over the ears, and the superb wings that complete his equipment to obey the noble impulse of home-love. Now the mental and physical equipments of the last lot of young birds were to be put to test.

Although there were plenty of witnesses, I thought it best to close all but one of the pigeon-doors and stand ready to shut that behind the first arrival.

I shall never forget the sensations of that day. I had been warned: "They start at 12; they should be here at 12:30; but look out, they come like a whirlwind. You hardly see them till they're in."

We were ranged along the inside of the loft, each with an eye to a crack or a partly closed pigeon-door, anxiously scanning the southwestern horizon, when one shouted: "Look out —here they come!" Like a white cloud they burst into view, low skimming over the city roofs, around a great chimney pile, and in two seconds after first being seen they were back. The flash of white, the rush of pinions, were all so sudden, so short, that, though preparing, I was unprepared. I was at the only open door. A whistling arrow of blue shot in, lashed my face with its pinions, and passed. I had hardly time to drop the little door, as a yell burst from the men, "Arnaux! Arnaux! I told you he would. Oh, he's a darling; only three months old and a winner—he's a little darling!" and Arnaux's owner danced, more for joy in his bird than in the purse he had won.

The men sat or kneeled and watched him in positive reverence as he gulped a quantity of water, then turned to the food-trough.

"Look at that eye, those wings, and did you ever see such a breast? Oh, but he's the real grit!" so his owner prattled to the silent ones whose birds had been defeated.

That was the first of Arnaux's exploits. Best of fifty birds from a good loft, his future was bright with promise.

He was invested with the silver anklet of the Sacred Order of the High Homer. It bore his number, 2590 C, a number which to-day means much to all men in the world of the Homing Pigeon.

In that trial flight from Elizabeth only forty birds had returned. It is usually so. Some were weak and got left behind, some were foolish and strayed. By this simple process of flight selection the pigeon-owners keep improving their stock. Of the ten, five were seen no more, but five returned later that day, not all at once, but straggling in; the last of the loiterers was a big, lubberly Blue Pigeon. The man in the loft at the time called: "Here comes that old sapheaded Blue that Jakey was betting on. I didn't suppose he would come back, and didn't care, neither, for it's my belief he has a streak of Pouter."

The Big Blue, also called "Corner-box" from the nest where he was hatched, had shown remarkable vigor from the first. Though all were about the same age, he had grown faster, was bigger, and incidentally handsomer, though the fanciers cared little for that. He seemed fully aware of his importance, and early showed a disposition to bully his smaller cousins. His owner prophesied great things of him, but Billy, the stable-man, had grave doubts over the length of his neck, the bigness of his crop, his carriage, and his over-size. "A bird can't make time pushing a bag of wind ahead of him. Them long legs is dead weight, an' a neck like that ain't got no gimp in it," Billy would grunt disparagingly as he cleaned out the loft of a morning.

2

The training of the birds went on after this at regular times. The distance from home, of the start, was "jumped" twenty-five or thirty miles farther each day, and its direction changed till the Homers knew the country for one hundred and fifty miles around New York. The original birds dwindled to twenty, for the rigid process weeds out not only the weak and ill-equipped, but those also who may have temporary ailments or accidents, or who may make the mistake of overeating at the start. There were many fine birds in that flight, broad-breasted, bright-eyed, long-winged creatures, formed for swiftest flight, for high unconscious emprise, for these were destined to be messengers in the service of man in times of serious need. Their colors were mostly white, blue, or brown. They wore no uniform, but each and all of the chosen remnant had the brilliant eye and the bulging ears of the finest Homer blood; and, best and choicest of all, nearly always first among them was little Arnaux. He had not much to distinguish him when at rest, for now all of the band had the silver anklet, but in the air it was that Arnaux showed his make, and when the opening of the hamper gave the order "Start," it was Arnaux that first got under way, soared to the height deemed needful to exclude all local influence, divined the road to home, and took it, pausing not for food, drink, or company.

Notwithstanding Billy's evil forecasts, the Big Blue of the Corner-box was one of the chosen twenty. Often he was late in returning; he never was first, and sometimes when he came back hours behind the rest, it was plain that he was neither hungry nor thirsty, sure signs that he was a loiterer by the way. Still he had come back; and now he wore on his ankle, like the rest, the sacred badge and a number from the roll of possible fame. Billy despised him, set him in poor contrast with Arnaux, but his owner would reply: "Give him a chance; 'soon ripe, soon rotten,' an' I always notice the best bird is the slowest to show up at first."

Before a year little Arnaux had made a record. The hardest

of all work is over the sea, for there is no chance of aid from landmarks; and the hardest of all times at sea is in fog, for then even the sun is blotted out and there is nothing whatever for guidance. With memory, sight, and hearing unavailable, the Homer has one thing left, and herein is his great strength, the inborn sense of direction. There is only one thing that can destroy this, and that is *fear*, hence the necessity of a stout little heart between those noble wings.

Arnaux, with two of his order, in course of training, had been shipped on an ocean steamer bound for Europe. They were to be released out of sight of land, but a heavy fog set in and forbade the start. The steamer took them onward, the intention being to send them back with the next vessel. When ten hours out the engine broke down, the fog settled dense over the sea, and the vessel was adrift and helpless as a log. She could only whistle for assistance, and so far as results were concerned, the captain might as well have wigwagged. Then the Pigeons were thought of. Starback, 2592 C, was first selected. A message for help was written on waterproof paper, rolled up, and lashed to his tail-feathers on the under side. He was thrown into the air and disappeared. Half an hour later, a second, the Big Blue Corner-box, 2600 C, was freighted with a letter. He flew up, but almost immediately returned and alighted on the rigging. He was a picture of pigeon fear; nothing could induce him to leave the ship. He was so terrorized that he was easily caught and ignominiously thrust back into the coop.

Now the third was brought out, a small, chunky bird. The shipmen did not know him, but they noted down from his anklet his name and number, Arnaux, 2590 C. It meant nothing to them. But the officer who held him noted that his heart did not beat so wildly as that of the last bird. The message was taken from the Big Blue. It ran:

10 A.M., Tuesday.

We broke our shaft two hundred and ten miles out from New York; we are drifting helplessly in the fog. Send out a tug as soon as possible. We are whistling one long, followed at once by one short, every sixty seconds.

(Signed)   THE CAPTAIN.

This was rolled up, wrapped in waterproof film, addressed to the Steamship Company, and lashed to the under side of Arnaux's middle tail-feather.

When thrown into the air, he circled round the ship, then round again higher, then again higher in a wider circle, and he was lost to view; and still higher till quite out of sight and feeling of the ship. Shut out from the use of all his senses now but one, he gave himself up to that. Strong in him it was, and untrammelled of that murderous despot *Fear*. True as a needle to the Pole went Arnaux now, no hesitation, no doubts; within one minute of leaving the coop he was speeding straight as a ray of light for the loft where he was born, the only place on earth where he could be made content.

That afternoon Billy was on duty when the whistle of fast wings was heard; a blue Flyer flashed into the loft and made for the water-trough. He was gulping down mouthful after mouthful, when Billy gasped: "Why, Arnaux, it's you, you beauty." Then, with the quick habit of the pigeon-man, he pulled out his watch and marked the time, 2:40 P.M. A glance showed the tie string on the tail. He shut the door and dropped the catching-net quickly over Arnaux's head. A moment later he had the roll in his hand; in two minutes he was speeding to the office of the Company, for there was a fat tip in view. There he learned that Arnaux had made the two hundred and ten miles in fog, over sea, in four hours and forty minutes, and within one hour the needful help had set out for the unfortunate steamer.

Two hundred and ten miles in fog over sea in four hours and forty minutes! This was a noble record. It was duly inscribed in the rolls of the Homing Club. Arnaux was held while the secretary, with rubber stamp and indelible ink, printed on a snowy primary of his right wing the record of the feat, with the date and reference number.

Starback, the second bird, never was heard of again. No doubt he perished at sea.

Blue Corner-box came back on the tug.

3

That was Arnaux's first public record; but others came fast, and several curious scenes were enacted in that old pigeon-loft with Arnaux as the central figure. One day a carriage drove up to the stable; a white-haired gentleman got out, climbed the dusty stairs, and sat all morning in the loft with Billy. Peering from his gold-rimmed glasses, first at a lot of papers, next across the roofs of the city, waiting, watching, for what? News from a little place not forty miles away— news of greatest weight to him, tidings that would make or break him, tidings that must reach him before it could be telegraphed: a telegram meant at least an hour's delay at each end. What was faster than that for forty miles? In those days there was but one thing—a high-class Homer. Money would count for nothing if he could win. The best, the very best at any price he must have, and Arnaux, with seven indelible records on his pinions, was the chosen messenger. An hour went by, another, and a third was begun, when with whistle of wings, the blue meteor flashed into the loft. Billy slammed the door and caught him. Deftly he snipped the threads and handed the roll to the banker. The old man turned deathly pale, fumbled it open, then his color came back. "Thank God!" he gasped, and then went speeding to his Board meeting, master of the situation. Little Arnaux has saved him.

The banker wanted to buy the Homer, feeling in a vague way that he ought to honor and cherish him; but Billy was very clear about it. "What's the good? You can't buy a Homer's heart. You could keep him a prisoner, that's all; but nothing on earth could make him forsake the old loft where he was hatched." So Arnaux stayed at 211 West Nineteenth Street. But the banker did not forget.

There is in our country a class of miscreants who think a flying Pigeon is fair game, because it is probably far from home, or they shoot him because it is hard to fix the crime. Many a noble Homer, speeding with a life or death message, has been shot down by one of the wretches and remorselessly made into a pot-pie. Arnaux's brother Arnolf, with three fine records on his wings, was thus murdered in the act of bearing a hasty summons for the doctor. As he fell dying at the gunner's feet, his superb wings spread out displayed his list of victories. The silver badge on his leg was there, and the gunner was smitten with remorse. He had the message sent on; he returned the dead bird to the Homing Club, saying that he "found it." The owner came to see him; the gunner broke down under cross-examination, and was forced to admit that he himself had shot the Homer, but did so in behalf of a poor sick neighbor who craved a pigeon-pie.

There were tears in the wrath of the pigeon-man. "My bird, my beautiful Arnolf, twenty times has he brought vital messages, three times has he made records, twice has he saved human lives, and you'd shoot him for a pot-pie. I could punish you under the law, but I have no heart for such a poor revenge. I only ask you this, if ever again you have a sick neighbor who wants a pigeon-pie, come, we'll freely supply him with pie-breed squabs; but if you have a trace of manhood about you, you will never, never again shoot, or allow others to shoot, our noble and priceless messengers."

This took place while the banker was in touch with the loft, while his heart was warm for the Pigeons. He was a man of influence, and the Pigeon Protective legislation at Albany was the immediate fruit of Arnaux's exploit.

THE MESSENGER of MERCY

4

Billy had never liked the Corner-box Blue (2600 C); notwithstanding the fact that he still continued in the ranks of the Silver Badge, Billy believed he was poor stuff. The steamer incident seemed to prove him a coward; he certainly was a bully.

One morning when Billy went in there was a row, two Pigeons, a large and a small, alternately clinching and sparring all over the floor, feathers flying, dust and commotion everywhere. As soon as they were separated Billy found that the little one was Arnaux and the big one was the Corner-box

Blue. Arnaux had made a good fight, but was overmatched, for the Big Blue was half as heavy again.

Soon it was very clear what they had fought over—a pretty little lady Pigeon of the bluest Homing blood. The Big Blue cock had kept up a state of bad feeling by his bullying, but it was the Little Lady that had made them close in mortal combat. Billy had no authority to wring the Big Blue's neck, but he interfered as far as he could in behalf of his favorite Arnaux.

Pigeon marriages are arranged somewhat like those of mankind. Propinquity is the first thing: force the pair together for a time and let nature take its course. So Billy locked Arnaux and the Little Lady up together in a separate apartment for two weeks, and to make doubly sure he locked Big Blue up with an Available Lady in another apartment for two weeks.

Things turned out just as was expected. The Little Lady surrendered to Arnaux and the Available Lady to the Big Blue. Two nests were begun and everything shaped for a "lived happily ever after." But the Big Blue was very big and handsome. He could blow out his crop and strut in the sun and make rainbows all round his neck in a way that might turn the heart of the staidest Homerine.

Arnaux, though sturdily built, was small and except for his brilliant eyes, not especially good-looking. Moreover, he was often away on important business, and the Big Blue had nothing to do but stay around the loft and display his unlettered wings.

It is the custom of moralists to point to the lower animals, and especially to the Pigeon, for examples of love and constancy, and properly so, but, alas! there are exceptions. Vice is not by any means limited to the human race.

Anaux's wife had been deeply impressed with the Big Blue, at the outset, and at length while her spouse was absent the dreadful thing took place.

Arnaux returned from Boston one day to find that the Big Blue, while he retained his own Available Lady in the corner-box, had also annexed the box and wife that belonged to himself, and a desperate battle followed. The only spectators were the two wives, but they maintained an indifferent aloofness. Arnaux fought with his famous wings, but they were none the better weapons because they now bore twenty records. His beak and feet were small, as became his blood, and his stout little heart could not make up for his lack of weight. The battle went against him. His wife sat unconcernedly in the nest, as though it were not her affair, and Arnaux might have been killed but for the timely arrival of Billy. He was angry enough to wring the Blue bird's neck, but the bully escaped from the loft in time. Billy took tender care of Arnaux for a few days. At the end of a week he was well again, and in ten days he was once more on the road. Meanwhile he had evidently forgiven his faithless wife, for, without any apparent feeling, he took up his nesting as before. That month he made two new records. He brought a message ten miles in eight minutes, and he came from Boston in four hours. Every moment of the way he had been impelled by the master-passion of home-love. But it was a poor home-coming if his wife figured at all in his thoughts, for he found her again flirting with the Big Blue cock. Tired as he was, the duel was renewed, and again would have been to a finish but for Billy's interference. He separated the fighters, then shut the Blue cock up in a coop, determined to get rid of him in some way. Meanwhile the "Any Age Sweepstakes" handicap from Chicago to New York was on, a race of nine hundred miles. Arnaux had been entered six months before. His forfeit-money was up, and notwithstanding his domestic complications, his friends felt that he must not fail to appear.

The birds were sent by train to Chicago, to be liberated at intervals there according to their handicap, and last of the start was Arnaux. They lost no time, and outside of Chicago several of these prime Flyers joined by common impulse into a racing flock that went through air on the same invisible track. A Homer may make a straight line when following his general sense of direction, but when following a familiar back track he sticks to the well-remembered landmarks. Most of the birds had been trained by way of Columbus and Buffalo. Arnaux knew the Columbus route, but also he knew that by Detroit, and after leaving Lake Michigan, he took the straight line for Detroit. Thus he caught up on his handicap and had the advantage of many miles. Detroit, Buffalo, Rochester, with their familiar towers and chimneys, faded behind him, and Syracuse was near at hand. It was now late afternoon; six hundred miles in twelve hours he had flown and was undoubtedly leading the race; but the usual thirst of the Flyer had attacked him. Skimming over the city roofs, he saw a loft of Pigeons, and descending from his high course in two or three great circles, he followed the ingoing Birds to the loft and drank greedily at the water-trough, as he had often done before, and as every pigeon-lover hospitably expects the messengers to do. The owner of the loft was there and noted the strange Bird. He stepped quietly to where he could inspect him. One of his own Pigeons made momentary opposition to the stranger, and Arnaux, sparring sidewise with an open wing in Pigeon style, displayed the long array of printed records. The man was a fancier. His interest was aroused; he pulled the string that shut the flying door, and in a few minutes Arnaux was his prisoner.

The robber spread the much-inscribed wings, read record after record, and glancing at the silver badge—it should have been gold—he read his name—Arnaux; then exclaimed: "Arnaux! Arnaux! Oh, I've heard of you, you little beauty, and it's glad I am to trap you." He snipped the message from his tail, unrolled it, and read: "Arnaux left Chicago this morning at 4 A.M., scratched in the Any Age Sweepstakes for New York."

"Six hundred miles in twelve hours! By the powers, that's a record-breaker." And the pigeon-stealer gently, almost reverently, put the fluttering Bird safely into a padded cage. "Well," he added, "I know it's no use trying to make you stay, but I can breed from you and have some of your strain."

So Arnaux was shut up in a large and comfortable loft with several other prisoners. The man, though a thief, was a lover of Homers; he gave his captive everything that could insure his comfort and safety. For three months he left him in that loft. At first Arnaux did nothing all day but walk up and down the wire screen, looking high and low for means of escape; but in the fouth month he seemed to have abandoned the attempt, and the watchful jailer began the second part of his scheme. He introduced a coy young lady Pigeon. But it did not seem to answer; Arnaux was not even civil to her. After a time the jailer removed the female, and Arnaux was left in solitary confinement for a month. Now a different female was brought in, but with no better luck; and thus it went on—for a year different charmers were introduced. Arnaux either violently repelled them or was scornfully indifferent, and at times the old longing to get away, came back with twofold power, so that he darted up and down the wire front or dashed with all his force against it.

When the storied feathers of his wings began their annual moult, his jailer saved them as precious things, and as each new feather came he reproduced on it the record of its owner's fame.

Two years went slowly by, and the jailer had put Arnaux in a new loft and brought in another lady Pigeon. By chance she closely resembled the faithless one at home. Arnaux actually heeded the newcomer. Once the jailer thought he saw his famous prisoner paying some slight attention to the charmer, and, yes, he surely saw her preparing a nest. Then assuming that they had reached a full understanding, the jailer, for the first time, opened the outlet, and Arnaux was free. Did he hang around in doubt? Did he hesitate? No, not for one moment. As soon as the drop of the door left open the way, he shot through, he spread those wonderful blazoned wings, and, with no second thought for the latest Circe, sprang from the hated prison loft—away and away.

5

We have no means of looking into the Pigeon's mind; we may go wrong in conjuring up for it deep thoughts of love and welcome home; but we are safe in this, we cannot too strongly paint, we cannot too highly praise and glorify that wonderful God-implanted, mankind-fostered home-love that glows unquenchably in this noble bird. Call it what you like, a mere instinct deliberately constructed by man for his self-fish ends, explain it away if you will, dissect it, misname it, and it still is there, in overwhelming, imperishable master-power, as long as the brave little heart and wings can beat.

Home, home, sweet home! Never had mankind a stronger love of home than Arnaux. The trials and sorrows of the old pigeon-loft were forgotten in that all-dominating force of his nature. Not years of prison bars, not later loves, nor fear of death, could down its power; and Arnaux, had the gift of song been his, must surely have sung as sings a hero in his highest joy, when sprang he from the 'lighting board, up-circling free, soaring, drawn by the only impulse that those glorious wings would honor,—up, up, in widening, heighten-ing circles of ashy blue in the blue, flashing those many-lettered wings of white, till they seemed like jets of fire—up and on, driven by that home-love, faithful to his only home and to his faithless mate; closing his eyes, they say; closing his ears, they tell; shutting his mind,—we all believe,—to nearer things, to two years of his life, to one half of his prime, but soaring in the blue, retiring, as a saint might do, into his inner self, giving himself up to that inmost guide. He was the captain of the ship, but the pilot, the chart and compass, all, were that deep-implanted instinct. One thousand feet above the trees the inscrutable whisper came, and Arnaux in arrowy swiftness now was pointing for the south-southeast. The little flashes of white fire on each side were lost in the low sky, and the reverent robber of Syracuse saw Arnaux nevermore.

The fast express was steaming down the valley. It was far ahead, but Arnaux overtook and passed it, as the flying wild Duck passes the swimming Muskrat. High in the valleys he went, low over the hills of Chenango, where the pines were combing the breezes.

Out from his oak-tree eyrie a Hawk came wheeling and sailing, silent, for he had marked the Flyer, and meant him for his prey. Arnaux turned neither right nor left, nor raised nor lowered his flight, nor lost a wing-beat. The Hawk was in waiting in the gap ahead, and Arnaux passed him, even as a Deer in his prime may pass a Bear in his pathway. Home! home! was the only burning thought, the blinding impulse.

Beat, beat, beat, those flashing pinions went with speed unslacked on the now familiar road. In an hour the Catskills were at hand. In two hours he was passing over them. Old friendly places, swiftly coming now, lent more force to his wings. Home! home! was the silent song that his heart was singing. Like the traveller dying of thirst, that sees the palm-trees far ahead, his brilliant eyes took in the distant smoke of Manhattan.

Out from the crest of the Catskills there launched a Falcon. Swiftest of the race of rapine, proud of his strength, proud of his wings, he rejoiced in a worthy prey. Many and many a Pigeon had been borne to his nest, and riding the wind he came, swooping, reserving his strength, awaiting the proper time. Oh, how well he knew the very moment! Down, down like a flashing javelin; no wild Duck, no Hawk could elude him, for this was a Falcon. Turn back now, O Homer, and save yourself; go round the dangerous hills. Did he turn? Not a whit! for this was Arnaux. Home! home! home! was his only thought. To meet the danger, he merely added to his speed; and the Peregrine stooped; stooped at what?—a flashing of color, a twinkling of whiteness—and went back empty. While Arnaux cleft the air of the valley as a stone from a sling, to be lost—a white-winged bird—a spot with flashing halo—and, quickly, a speck in the offing. On down the dear valley of Hudson, the well-known highway; for two years he had not seen it! Now he dropped low as the noon breeze came north and ruffled the river below him. Home! home! home! and the towers of a city are coming in view! Home! home! past the great spider-bridge of Poughkeepsie, skimming, skirting the river-banks. Low now by the bank as the wind arose. Low, alas! too low! What fiend was it tempted a gunner in June to lurk on that hill by the margin? what devil directed his gaze to the twinkling of white that came from the blue to the northward? Oh, Arnaux, Arnaux, skimming low, forget not the gunner of old! Too low, too low you are clearing that hill. Too low—*too late!* Flash—bang! and the death-hail has reached him; reached, maimed, but not downed him. Out of the flashing pinions broken feathers printed with records went fluttering earthward. The "naught" of his sea record was gone. Not two hundred and ten, but twenty-one miles it now read. Oh, shameful pillage! A dark stain appeared on his bosom, but Arnaux kept on. Home, home, homeward bound. The danger was past in an instant. Home, homeward he steered straight as before, but the wonderful speed was diminished; not a mile a minute now; and the wind made undue sounds in his tattered pinions. The stain in his breast told of broken force; but on, straight on, he flew. Home, home was in sight, and the pain in his breast was forgotten. The tall towers of the city were in clear view of his far-seeing eye as he skimmed by the high cliffs of Jersey. On, on—the pinion might flag, the eye might darken, but the home-love was stronger and stronger.

Under the tall Palisades, to be screened from the wind, he passed, over the sparkling water, over the trees, under the Peregrines' eyrie, under the pirates' castle where the great grim Peregrines sat; peering like black-masked highwaymen they marked the on-coming Pigeon. Arnaux knew them of old. Many a message was lying undelivered in that nest, many a record-bearing plume had fluttered away from its fastness. But Arnaux had faced them before, and now he came as before—on, onward, swift, but not as he had been; the deadly gun had sapped his force, had lowered his speed. On, on; and the Peregrines, biding their time, went forth like two bow-bolts; strong and lightning-swift they went against one weak and wearied.

Why tell of the race that followed? Why paint the despair of a brave little heart in sight of the home he had craved in vain? In a minute all was over. The Peregrines screeched in their triumph. Screeching and sailing, they swung to their eyrie, and the prey in their claws was the body, the last of the bright little Arnaux. There on the rocks the beaks and claws of the bandits were red with the life of the hero. Torn asunder were those matchless wings, and their records were scattered unnoticed. In sun and in storm they lay till the killers themselves were killed and their stronghold rifled. And none knew the fate of the peerless Bird till deep in the dust and rubbish of that pirate-nest the avenger found, among others of its kind, a silver ring, the sacred badge of the High Homer, and read upon it the pregnant inscription:

"ARNAUX, 2590 C."

Badlands Billy

Badlands Billy

1

THE HOWL BY NIGHT

O you know the three calls of the hunting Wolf:—the long-drawn deep howl, the muster, that tells of game discovered but too strong for the finder to manage alone; and the higher ululation that ringing and swelling is the cry of the pack on a hot scent; and the sharp bark coupled with a short howl that, seeming least of all, is yet a gong of doom, for this is the cry *"Close in"*—this is the finish?

We were riding the Badland Buttes, King and I, with a pack of various hunting Dogs stringing behind or trotting alongside. The sun had gone from the sky, and a blood-streak marked the spot where he died, away over Sentinel Butte. The hills were dim, the valleys dark, when from the nearest gloom there rolled a long-drawn cry that all men recognize instinctively—melodious, yet with a tone in it that sends a shudder up the spine, though now it has lost all menace for mankind. We listened for a moment. It was the Wolf-hunter who broke silence: "That's Badlands Billy; ain't it a voice? He's out for his beef tonight."

2

ANCIENT DAYS

In pristine days the Buffalo herds were followed by bands
of Wolves that preyed on the sick, the weak, and the wounded.
When the Buffalo were exterminated the Wolves were hard
put for support, but the Cattle came and solved the question
for them by taking the Buffaloes' place. This caused the wolf-
war. The ranchmen offered a bounty for each Wolf killed,
and every cowboy out of work was supplied with traps and
poison for wolf-killing. The very expert made this their sole
business and became known as wolvers. King Ryder was one
of these. He was a quiet, gentle-spoken fellow, with a keen
eye and an insight into animal life that gave him especial
power over Broncos and Dogs, as well as Wolves and Bears,
though in the last two cases it was power merely to surmise
where they were and how best to get at them. He had been
a wolver for years, and greatly surprised me by saying that
"never in all his experience had he known a Gray-wolf to
attack a human being."

We had many camp-fire talks while the other men were
sleeping, and then it was I learned the little that he knew
about Badlands Billy. "Six times have I seen him and the
seventh will be Sunday, you bet. He takes his long rest then."
And thus on the very ground where it all fell out, to the
noise of the night wind and the yapping of the Coyote, inter-
rupted sometimes by the deep-drawn howl of the hero himself, I heard chapters of this history which, with others gleaned
in many fields, gave me the story of the Big Dark Wolf of
Sentinel Butte.

3

IN THE CAÑON

Away back in the spring of '92 a wolver was "wolving" on the east side of the Sentinel Mountain that so long was a principal landmark of the old Plainsmen. Pelts were not good in May, but the bounties were high, five dollars a head, and double for She-wolves. As he went down to the creek one morning he saw a Wolf coming to drink on the other side. He had an easy shot, and on killing it found it was a nursing She-wolf. Evidently her family were somewhere near, so he spent two or three days searching in all the likely places, but found no clue to the den.

Two weeks afterward, as the wolver rode down an adjoining cañon, he saw a Wolf come out of a hole. The ever-ready rifle flew up, and another ten-dollar scalp was added to his string. Now he dug into the den and found the litter, a most surprising one indeed, for it consisted not of the usual five or six Wolf-pups, but of eleven, and these, strange to say, were of two sizes, five of them larger and older than the other six. Here were two distinct families with one mother, and as he added their scalps to his string of trophies the truth dawned on the hunter. One lot was surely the family of the She-wolf he had killed two weeks before. The case was clear: the little ones awaiting the mother that was never to come, had whined piteously and more loudly as their hunger-pangs increased; the other mother passing had heard the Cubs; her heart was tender now, her own little ones had so recently come, and she cared for the orphans, carried them to her own den, and was providing for the double family when the rifleman had cut the gentle chapter short.

Many a wolver has dug into a wolf-den to find nothing. The old Wolves or possibly the Cubs themselves often dig little side pockets and off galleries, and when an enemy is breaking in they hide in these. The loose earth conceals the small pocket and thus the Cubs escape. When the wolver retired with his scalps he did not know that the biggest of all the Cubs was still in the den, and even had he waited about for two hours, he might have been no wiser. Three hours later the sun went down and there was a slight scratching afar in the hole; first two little gray paws, then a small black nose appeared in a soft sand-pile to one side of the den. At length the Cub came forth from his hiding. He had been frightened by the attack on the den; now he was perplexed by its condition.

It was thrice as large as it had been and open at the top now. Lying near were things that smelled like his brothers and sisters, but they were repellent to him. He was filled with fear as he sniffed at them, and sneaked aside into a thicket of grass, as a Night-hawk boomed over his head. He crouched all night in that thicket. He did not dare to go near the den, and knew not where else he could go. The next morning when two Vultures came swooping down on the bodies, the Wolf-cub ran off in the thicket, and seeking its deepest cover, was led down a ravine to a wide valley. Suddenly there arose from the grass a big She-wolf, like his mother, yet different, a stranger, and instinctively the stray Cub sank to the earth, as the old Wolf bounded on him. No doubt the Cub had been taken for some lawful prey, but a whiff set that right. She stood over him for an instant. He grovelled at her feet. The impulse to kill him or at least give

him a shake died away. He had the smell of a young Cub.
Her own were about his age, her heart was touched, and
when he found courage enough to put his nose up and smell
her nose, she made no angry demonstration except a short
half-hearted growl. Now, however, he had smelled something
that he sorely needed. He had not fed since the day before,
and when the old Wolf turned to leave him, he tumbled
after her on clumsy puppy legs. Had the Mother-wolf been
far from home he must soon have been left behind, but the
nearest hollow was the chosen place, and the Cub arrived
at the den's mouth soon after the Mother-wolf.

A stranger is an enemy, and the old one rushing forth
to the defense, met the Cub again, and again was restrained
by something that rose in her responsive to the smell. The
Cub had thrown himself on his back in utter submission, but
that did not prevent his nose reporting to him the good thing
almost within reach. The She-wolf went into the den and
curled herself about her brood; the Cub persisted in following. She snarled as he approached her own little ones, but
disarming wrath each time by submission and his very cub-
hood, he was presently among her brood, helping himself to
what he wanted so greatly, and thus he adopted himself into
her family. In a few days he was so much one of them that
the mother forgot about his being a stranger. Yet he was
different from them in several ways—older by two weeks,
stronger, and marked on the neck and shoulders with what
afterward grew to be a dark mane.

Little Duskymane could not have been happier in his choice
of a foster-mother, for the Yellow Wolf was not only a good
hunter with a fund of cunning, but she was a Wolf of modern
ideas as well. The old tricks of tolling a Prairie Dog, relaying

for Antelope, houghing a Bronco or flanking a Steer she had learned partly from instinct and partly from the example of her more experienced relatives, when they joined to form the winter bands. But, just as necessary nowadays, she had learned that all men carry guns, that guns are irresistible, that the only way to avoid them is by keeping out of sight while the sun is up, and yet that at night they are harmless. She had a fair comprehension of traps, indeed she had been in one once, and though she left a toe behind in pulling free, it was a toe most advantageously disposed of; thenceforth, though not comprehending the nature of the trap, she was thoroughly imbued with the horror of it, with the idea indeed that iron is dangerous, and at any price it should be avoided.

On one occasion, when she and five others were planning to raid a Sheep yard, she held back at the last minute because some new-strung wires appeared. The others rushed in to find the Sheep beyond their reach, themselves in a death-trap.

Thus she had learned the newer dangers, and while it is unlikely that she had any clear mental conception of them she had acquired a wholesome distrust of all things strange, and a horror of one or two in particular that proved her lasting safeguard. Each year she raised her brood successfully and the number of Yellow Wolves increased in the country. Guns, traps, men and the new animals they brought had been learned, but there was yet another lesson before her—a terrible one indeed.

About the time Duskymane's brothers were a month old his foster-mother returned in a strange condition. She was frothing at the mouth, her legs trembled, and she fell in a convulsion near the doorway of the den, but recovering, she came in. Her jaws quivered, her teeth rattled a little as she tried to lick

the little ones; she seized her own front leg and bit it so as not
to bite them, but at length she grew quieter and calmer. The
Cubs had retreated in fear to a far pocket, but now they returned and crowded about her to seek their usual food. The
mother recovered, but was very ill for two or three days, and
those days with the poison in her system worked disaster for
the brood. They were terribly sick; only the strongest could
survive, and when the trial of strength was over, the den contained only the old one and the Black-maned Cub, the one
she had adopted. Thus little Duskymane became her sole
charge; all her strength was devoted to feeding him, and he
thrived apace.

Wolves are quick to learn certain things. The reactions of
smell are the greatest that a Wolf can feel, and thenceforth
both Cub and foster-mother experienced a quick, unreasoning
sense of fear and hate the moment the smell of strychnine
reached them.

4

THE RUDIMENTS OF WOLF TRAINING

With the sustenance of seven at his service the little Wolf
had every reason to grow, and when in the autumn he began
to follow his mother on her hunting trips he was as tall as she
was. Now a change of region was forced on them, for numbers
of little Wolves were growing up. Sentinel Butte, the rocky
fastness of the plains, was claimed by many that were big and
strong; the weaker must move out, and with them Yellow
Wolf and the Dusky Cub.

Wolves have no language in the sense that man has; their

vocabulary is probably limited to a dozen howls, barks, and grunts expressing the simplest emotions; but they have several other modes of conveying ideas, and one very special method of spreading information—the Wolf-telephone. Scattered over their range are a number of recognized "centrals." Sometimes these are stones, sometimes the angle of cross-trails, sometimes a Buffalo-skull—indeed, any conspicuous object near a main trail is used. A Wolf calling here, as a Dog does at a telegraph post, or a Muskrat at a certain mud-pie point, leaves his body-scent and learns what other visitors have been there recently to do the same. He learns also whence they came and where they went, as well as something about their condition, whether hunted, hungry, gorged, or sick. By this system of registration a Wolf knows where his friends, as well as his foes, are to be found. And Duskymane, following after the Yellow Wolf, was taught the places and uses of the many signal-stations without any conscious attempt at teaching on the part of his foster-mother. Example backed by his native instincts was indeed the chief teacher, but on one occasion at least there was something very like the effort of a human parent to guard her child in danger.

The Dark Cub had learned the rudiments of Wolf life: that the way to fight Dogs is to run, and to fight as you run, never grapple, but snap, snap, snap, and make for the rough country where Horses cannot bring their riders.

He learned not to bother about the Coyotes that follow for the pickings when you hunt; you cannot catch them and they do you no harm.

He knew he must not waste time dashing after Birds that alight on the ground; and that he must keep away from the little black and white Animal with the bushy tail. It is not very good to eat, and it is very, very bad to smell.

Poison! Oh, he never forget that smell from the day when the den was cleared of all his foster-brothers.

He now knew that the first move in attacking Sheep was to scatter them; a lone Sheep is a foolish and easy prey; that the way to round up a band of Cattle was to frighten a Calf.

He learned that he must always attack a Steer behind, a Sheep in front, and a Horse in the middle, that is, on the flank, and never, never attack a man at all, never even face him. But an important lesson was added to these, one in which the mother consciously taught him of a secret foe.

5

THE LESSON ON TRAPS

A Calf had died in branding-time and now, two weeks later, was in its best state for perfect taste, not too fresh, not over-ripe—that is, in a Wolf's opinion—and the wind carried this information afar. The Yellow Wolf and Duskymane were out for supper, though not yet knowing where, when the tidings of veal arrived, and they trotted up the wind. The Calf was in an open place, and plain to be seen in the moonlight. A Dog would have trotted right up to the carcass, an old-time Wolf might have done so, but constant war had developed constant vigilance in the Yellow Wolf, and trusting nothing and no one but her nose, she slacked her speed to a walk. On coming in easy view she stopped, and for long swung her nose, submitting the wind to the closest possible chemical analysis. She tried it with her finest tests, blew all the membranes clean again and tried it once more; and this was the report of the trusty nostrils, yes, the unanimous report. First, rich and racy smell of Calf, seventy per cent.; smells of grass, bugs, wood, flowers, trees, sand, and other uninteresting negations, fifteen per cent.; smell of her Cub and herself, positive but ignorable, ten per cent.; smell of human tracks, two per cent.; smell of smoke, one per cent.; of sweaty leather smell, one per cent.; of human body-scent (not discernible in some samples), one-half per cent.; smell of iron, a trace.

The old Wolf crouched a little but sniffed hard with swinging nose; the young Wolf imitatively did the same. She backed off to a greater distance; the Cub stood. She gave a low whine; he followed unwillingly. She circled around the tempting carcass; a new smell was recorded—Coyote trail-scent, soon followed by Coyote body-scent. Yes, there they were sneaking along a near ridge, and now as she passed to one side the samples changed, the wind had lost nearly every trace of Calf; miscellaneous, commonplace, and uninteresting smells were there instead. The human track-scent was as before, the trace of leather was gone, but fully one-half per cent. of iron-odor, and body-smell of man raised to nearly two per cent.

Fully alarmed, she conveyed her fear to the Cub, by her rigid pose, her intent air, and her slightly bristling mane.

She continued her round. At one time on a high place the human body-scent was doubly strong, then as she dropped it faded. Then the wind brought the full calf-odor with several track-scents of Coyotes and sundry Birds. Her suspicions were lulling as in a smalling circle she neared the tempting feast from the windward side. She had even advanced straight toward it for a few steps when the sweaty leather sang loud and strong again, and smoke and iron mingled like two strands of a parti-colored yarn. Centering all her attention on this, she advanced within two leaps of the Calf. There on the ground was a scrap of leather, telling also of a human touch, close at hand the Calf, and now the iron and smoke on the full vast smell of Calf were like a snake trail across the trail of a whole Beef herd. It was so slight that the Cub, with the appetite and impatience of youth, pressed up against his mother's shoulder to go past and eat without delay. She seized him by the neck and flung him back. A stone struck by his feet rolled forward and stopped with a peculiar clink. The danger smell was greatly increased at this, and the Yellow Wolf backed slowly from the feast, the Cub unwillingly following.

As he looked wistfully he saw the Coyotes drawing nearer, mindful chiefly to avoid the Wolves. He watched their really cautious advance; it seemed like heedless rushing compared with his mother's approach. The Calf smell rolled forth in exquisite and overpowering excellence now, for they were tearing the meat, when a sharp clank was heard and a yelp from a Coyote. At the same time the quiet night was shocked with a roar and a flash of fire. Heavy shots spattered Calf and Coyotes, and yelping like beaten Dogs they scattered, excepting one that was killed and a second struggling in the trap set here by the ever-active wolvers. The air was charged with the hateful smells redoubled now, and horrid smells additional. The Yellow Wolf glided down a hollow and led her Cub away in flight, but, as they went, they saw a man rush from the bank near where the mother's nose had warned her of the human scent. They saw him kill the caught Coyote and set the traps for more.

6

THE BEGUILING OF THE YELLOW WOLF

The life game is a hard game, for we may win ten thousand times, and if we fail but once our gain is gone. How many hundred times had the Yellow Wolf scorned the traps; how many Cubs had she trained to do the same! Of all the dangers to her life she best knew traps.

October had come; the Cub was now much taller than the mother. The wolver had seen them once—a Yellow Wolf followed by another, whose long, awkward legs, big, soft feet, thin neck, and skimpy tail proclaimed him this year's Cub. The record of the dust and sand said that the old one had lost a right front toe, and that the young one was of giant size.

It was the wolver that thought to turn the carcass of the Calf to profit, but he was disappointed in getting Coyotes instead of Wolves. It was the beginning of the trapping season, for this month fur is prime. A young trapper often fastens the bait on the trap; an experienced one does not. A good trapper will even put the bait at one place and the trap ten or twenty feet away, but at a spot that the Wolf is likely to cross in circling. A favorite plan is to hide three or four traps around an open place, and scatter some scraps of meat in the middle. The traps are buried out of sight after being smoked to hide the taint of hands and iron. Sometimes no bait is used except a little piece of cotton or a tuft of feathers that may catch the Wolf's eye or pique its curiosity and tempt it to circle on the fateful, treacherous ground. A good trapper varies his methods continually so that the Wolves cannot learn his ways. Their only safeguards are perpetual vigilance and distrust of all smells that are known to be of man.

The wolver, with a load of the strongest steel traps, had begun his autumn work on the 'Cottonwood.'

An old Buffalo trail crossing the river followed a little draw that climbed the hills to the level upland. All animals use these trails, Wolves and Foxes as well as Cattle and Deer: they are the main thoroughfares. A cottonwood stump not far from where it plunged to the gravelly stream was marked with Wolf signs that told the wolver of its use. Here was an excellent place for traps, not on the trail, for Cattle were here in numbers, but twenty yards away on a level, sandy spot he set four traps in a twelve-foot square. Near each he scattered two or three scraps of meat; three or four white feathers on a spear of grass in the middle completed the setting. No human eye, few animal noses, could have detected the hidden danger of that sandy ground, when the sun and wind and the sand itself had dissipated the man-track taint.

The Yellow Wolf had seen and passed, and taught her giant son to pass, such traps a thousand times before.

The Cattle came to water in the heat of the day. They strung down the Buffalo path as once the Buffalo did. The little Vesper-birds flitted before them, the Cowbirds rode on them, and the Prairie-dogs chattered at them, just as they once did at the Buffalo.

Down from the gray-green mesa with its green-grays rocks, they marched with imposing solemnity, importance, and directness of purpose. Some frolicsome Calves, playing alongside the trail, grew sober and walked behind their mothers as the river flat was reached. The old Cow that headed the procession sniffed suspiciously as she passed the "trap set," but it was far away, otherwise she would have pawed and bellowed over the scraps of bloody beef till every trap was sprung and harmless.

But she led to the river. After all had drunk their fill they lay down on the nearest bank till late afternoon. Then their unheard dinner-gong aroused them, and started them on the backward march to where the richest pastures grew.

One or two small birds had picked at the scraps of meat, some blue-bottle flies buzzed about, but the sinking sun saw the sandy mask untouched.

A brown Marsh Hawk came skimming over the river flat as the sun began his color play. Blackbirds dashed into thickets, and easily avoided his clumsy pounce. It was too early for the Mice, but, as he skimmed the ground, his keen eye caught the flutter of feathers by the trap and turned his flight. The feathers in their uninteresting emptiness were exposed before he was near, but now he saw the scraps of meat. Guileless of cunning, he alighted and was devouring a second lump when—*clank*—the dust was flirted high and the Marsh Hawk was held by his toes, struggling vainly in the jaws of a powerful wolf-trap. He was not much hurt. His ample wings winnowed from time to time, in efforts to be free, but he was helpless, even as a Sparrow might be in a rat-trap, and when the sun had played his fierce chromatic scale, his swan-song sung, and died as he dies only in the blazing west, and the shades had fallen on the melodramatic scene of the Mouse in the elephant-trap, there was a deep, rich sound on the high flat butte, answered by another, neither very long, neither repeated, and both instinctive rather than necessary. One was the muster-call of an ordinary Wolf, the other the answer of a very big male, not a pair in this case, but mother and son—Yellow Wolf and Duskymane. They came trotting together down the

Buffalo trail. They paused at the telephone box on the hill and again at the old cottonwood root, and were making for the river when the Hawk in the trap fluttered his wings. The old Wolf turned toward him,—a wounded bird on the ground surely, and she rushed forward. Sun and sand soon burn all trail-scents; there was nothing to warn her. She sprang on the flopping bird and a chop of her jaws ended his troubles, but a horrid sound—the gritting of her teeth on steel—told her of peril. She dropped the Hawk and sprang backward from the dangerous ground, but landed in the second trap. High on her foot its death-grip closed, and leaping with all her strength, to escape, she set her fore foot in another of the lurking grips of steel. Never had a trap been so baited before. Never was she so unsuspicious. Never was catch more sure. Fear and fury filled the old Wolf's heart; she tugged and strained, she chewed the chains, she snarled and foamed. One trap with its buried log, she might have dragged; with two, she was helpless. Struggle as she might, it only worked those relentless jaws more deeply into her feet. She snapped wildly at the air; she tore the dead Hawk into shreds; she roared the short, barking roar of a crazy Wolf. She bit at the traps, at her cub, at herself. She tore her legs that were held; she gnawed in frenzy at her flank, she chopped off her tail in her madness; she splintered all her teeth on the steel, and filled her bleeding, foaming jaws with clay and sand.

She struggled till she fell, and writhed about or lay like dead, till strong enough to rise and grind the chains again with her teeth.

And so the night passed by.

And Duskymane? Where was he? The feeling of the time when his foster-mother had come home poisoned, now returned; but he was even more afraid of her. She seemed filled with fighting hate. He held away and whined a little; he slunk off and came back when she lay still, only to retreat again, as she sprang forward, raging at him, and then renewed her efforts at the traps. He did not understand it, but he knew this much, she was in terrible trouble, and the cause seemed to be the same as that which had scared them the night they had ventured near the Calf.

Duskymane hung about all night, fearing to go near, not knowing what to do, and helpless as his mother.

At dawn the next day a sheepherder seeking lost Sheep discovered her from a neighboring hill. A signal mirror called the wolver from his camp. Duskymane saw the new danger. He was a mere Cub, though so tall; he could not face the man, and fled at his approach.

The wolver rode up to the sorry, tattered, bleeding She-wolf in the trap. He raised his rifle and soon the struggling stopped.

The wolver read the trail and the signs about, and remembering those he had read before, he divined that this was the Wolf with the great Cub—the She-wolf of Sentinel Butte.

Duskymane heard the "crack" as he scurried off into cover. He could scarcely know what it meant, but he never saw his kind old foster-mother again. Thenceforth he must face the world alone.

7

THE YOUNG WOLF WINS A PLACE AND FAME

Instinct is no doubt a Wolf's first and best guide, but gifted parents are a great start in life. The dusky-maned cub had had a mother of rare excellence and he reaped the advantage of all her cleverness. He had inherited an exquisite nose and had absolute confidence in its admonitions. Mankind has difficulty in recognizing the power of nostrils. A Gray-wolf can glance over the morning wind as a man does over his newspaper, and get all the latest news. He can swing over the ground and have the minutest information of every living creature that has walked there within many hours. His nose even tells which way it ran, and in a word renders a statement of every animal that recently crossed his trail, whence it came, and whither it went.

That power had Duskymane in the highest degree; his broad, moist nose was evidence of it to all who are judges of such things. Added to this, his frame was of unusual power and endurance, and last, he had early learned a deep distrust of everything strange, and, call it what we will, shyness, wariness or suspicion, it was worth more to him than all his cleverness. It was this as much as his physical powers that made a success of his life. Might is right in wolf-land, and Duskymane and his mother had been driven out of Sentinel Butte. But it was a very delectable land and he kept drifting back to his native mountain. One or two big Wolves there resented his coming. They drove him off several times, yet each time he returned he was better able to face them; and before he was eighteen months old he had defeated all rivals and established himself again on his native ground; where he lived like a robber baron, levying tribute on the rich lands about him and finding safety in the rocky fastness.

Wolver Ryder often hunted in that country, and before long, he came across a five-and-one-half-inch track, the footprint of a giant Wolf. Roughly reckoned, twenty to twenty-

five pounds of weight or six inches of stature is a fair allow-
ance for each inch of a Wolf's foot; this Wolf therefore stood
thirty-three inches at the shoulder and weighed about one
hundred and forty pounds, by far the largest Wolf he had ever
met. King had lived in Goat country, and now in Goat language he exclaimed: "You bet, ain't that an old Billy?" Thus
by trivial chance it was that Duskymane was known to his foe
as 'Badlands Billy.'

Ryder was familiar with the muster-call of the Wolves, the
long, smooth cry, but Billy's had a singular feature, a slurring
that was always distinctive. Ryder had heard this before, in
the Cottonwood Cañon, and when at length he got a sight of
the big Wolf with the black mane, it struck him that this was
also the Cub of the old Yellow fury that he had trapped.

These were among the things he told me as we sat by the
fire at night. I knew of the early days when any one could trap
or poison Wolves, of the passing of those days, with the passing of the simple Wolves; of the new race of Wolves with new
cunning that were defying the methods of the ranchmen, and
increasing steadily in numbers. Now the wolver told me of the
various ventures that Penroof had made with different kinds
of Hounds: of Foxhounds too thin-skinned to fight; of Greyhounds that were useless when the animal was out of sight; of
Danes too heavy for the rough country, and, last, of the composite pack with some of all kinds, including at times a Bull-
terrier to lead them in the final fight.

He told of hunts after Coyotes, which usually were successful because the Coyotes sought the plains, and were easily
caught by the Greyhounds. He told of killing some small
Gray-wolves with this very pack, usually at the cost of the one
that led them; but above all he dwelt on the wonderful
prowess of "that thar cussed old Black Wolf of Sentinel

Butte," and related the many attempts to run him down or corner him—an unbroken array of failures. For the big Wolf, with exasperating persistence, continued to live on the finest stock of the Penroof brand, and each year was teaching more Wolves how to do the same with perfect impunity.

I listened even as gold-hunters listen to stories of treasure trove, for these were the things of my world. These things indeed were uppermost in all our minds, for the Penroof pack was lying around our camp-fire now. We were out after Badlands Billy.

8

THE VOICE IN THE NIGHT AND THE BIG TRACK IN THE MORNING

One night late in September after the last streak of light was gone from the west and the Coyotes had begun their yapping chorus, a deep, booming sound was heard. King took out his pipe, turned his head and said: "That's him—that's old Billy. He's been watching us all day from some high place, and now when the guns are useless he's here to have a little fun with us."

Two or three Dogs arose, with bristling manes, for they clearly recognized that this was no Coyote. They rushed out into the night, but did not go far; their brawling sounds were suddenly varied by loud yelps, and they came running back to the shelter of the fire. One was so badly cut in the shoulder that he was useless for the rest of the hunt. Another was hurt in the flank—it seemed the less serious wound, and yet next morning the hunters buried that second Dog.

The men were furious. They vowed speedy vengeance, and at dawn were off on the trail. The Coyotes yelped their dawning song, but they melted into the hills when the light was strong. The hunters searched about for the big Wolf's track, hoping that the Hounds would be able to take it up and find him, but they either could not or would not.

They found a Coyote, however, and within a few hundred yards they killed him. It was a victory, I suppose, for Coyotes kill Calves and Sheep, but somehow I felt the common thought of all: "Mighty brave Dogs for a little Coyote, but they could not face the big Wolf last night."

Young Penroof, as though in answer to one of the unput questions, said:

"Say, boys, I believe old Billy had a hull bunch of Wolves with him last night."

"Didn't see but one track," said King gruffly.

In this way the whole of October slipped by; all day hard riding after doubtful trails, following the Dogs, who either could not keep the big trail or feared to do so, and again and again we had news of damage done by the Wolf; sometimes a cowboy would report it to us; and sometimes we found the carcasses ourselves. A few of these we poisoned, though it is considered a very dangerous thing to do while running Dogs. The end of the month found us a weather-beaten, dispirited lot of men, with a worn-out lot of Horses, and a footsore pack, reduced in numbers from ten to seven. So far we had killed only one Gray-wolf and three Coyotes; Badlands Billy had killed at least a dozen Cows and Dogs at fifty dollars a head. Some of the boys decided to give it up and go home, so King took advantage of their going, to send a letter, asking for reënforcements including all the spare Dogs at the ranch.

During the two days' wait we rested our Horses, shot some game, and prepared for a harder hunt. Late on the second day the new Dogs arrived—eight beauties—and raised the working pack to fifteen.

The weather now turned much cooler, and in the morning, to the joy of the wolvers, the ground was white with snow. This surely meant success. With cool weather for the Dogs and Horses to run; with the big Wolf not far away, for he had been heard the night before; and with tracking snow, so that once found he could not baffle us,—escape for him was impossible.

We were up at dawn, but before we could get away, three men came riding into camp. They were the Penroof boys back again. The change of weather had changed their minds; they knew that with snow we might have luck.

"Remember now," said King, as all were mounting, "we don't want any but Badlands Billy this trip. Get him an' we kin bust up the hull combination. It is a five-and-a-half-inch track."

And each measured off on his quirt handle, or on his glove, the exact five and a half inches that was to be used in testing the tracks he might find.

Not more than an hour elapsed before we got a signal from the rider who had gone westward. One shot: that means "attention," a pause while counting ten, then two shots: that means *"come on."*

King gathered the Dogs and rode direct to the distant figure on the hill. All hearts beat high with hope, and we were not disappointed. Some small Wolf tracks had been found, but here at last was the big track, nearly six inches long. Young Penroof wanted to yell and set out at full gallop. It was like hunting a Lion; it was like finding happiness long deferred. The hunter knows nothing more inspiring than the clean-cut line of fresh tracks that is leading to a wonderful animal he has long been hunting in vain. How King's eye gleamed as he gloated over the sign!

9

RUN DOWN AT LAST

It was the roughest of all rough riding. It was a far longer hunt than we had expected, and was full of little incidents, for that endless line of marks was a minute history of all that the big Wolf had done the night before. Here he had circled at the telephone box and looked for news; there he had paused to examine an old skull; here he had shied off and swung cautiously up wind to examine something that proved to be an old tin can; there at length he had mounted a low hill and sat down, probably giving the muster-howl, for two Wolves had come to him from different directions, and they then had descended to the river flat where the Cattle would seek shelter during the storm. Here all three had visited a Buffalo skull; there they trotted in line; and yonder they separated, going three different ways, to meet—yes—here—oh, what a sight, a fine Cow ripped open, left dead and *uneaten*. Not to their taste, it seems, for see! within a mile is another killed by them. Not six hours ago, they had feasted. Here their trails scatter again, but not far, and the snow tells plainly how each had lain down to sleep. The Hounds' manes bristled as they sniffed those places. King had held the Dogs well in hand, but now they were greatly excited. We came to a hill whereon the Wolves had turned and faced our way, then fled at full speed, —so said the trail,—and now it was clear that they had watched us from that hill, and were not far away.

The pack kept well together, because the Greyhounds, seeing no quarry, were merely puttering about among the other Dogs, or running back with the Horses. We went as fast as we could, for the Wolves were speeding. Up mesas and down coulees we rode, sticking closely to the Dogs, though it was the roughest country that could be picked. One gully after another, an hour and another hour, and still the threefold track went bounding on; another hour and no change, but interminable climbing, sliding, struggling, through brush and over boulders, guided by the far-away yelping of the Dogs.

Now the chase led downward to the low valley of the river, where there was scarcely any snow. Jumping and scrambling down hills, recklessly leaping dangerous gullies and slippery rocks, we felt that we could not hold out much longer; when on the lowest, dryest level the pack split, some went up, some went down, and others straight on. Oh, how King did swear! He knew at once what it meant. The Wolves had scattered, and so had divided the pack. Three Dogs after a Wolf would have no chance, four could not kill him, two would certainly be killed. And yet this was the first encouraging sign we had seen, for it meant that the Wolves were hard pressed. We spurred ahead to stop the Dogs, to pick for them the only trail. But that was not so easy. Without snow here and with countless Dog tracks, we were foiled. All we could do was to let the Dogs choose, but keep them to a single choice. Away we went as before, hoping, yet fearing that we were not on the right track. The Dogs ran well, very fast indeed. This was a bad sign, King said, but we could not get sight of the track because the Dogs overran it before we came.

After a two-mile run the chase led upward again in snow country; the Wolf was sighted, but to our disgust, we were on the track of the smallest one.

"I thought so," growled young Penroof. "Dogs was altogether too keen for a serious proposition. Kind o' surprised it ain't turned out a Jack-rabbit."

Within another mile he had turned to bay in a willow thicket. We heard him howl the long-drawn howl for help, and before we could reach the place King saw the dogs recoil and scatter. A minute later there sped from the far side of the thicket a small Gray-wolf and a Black One of very much greater size.

"By golly, if he didn't yell for help, and Billy come back to help him; that's great!" exclaimed the wolver. And my heart went out to the brave old Wolf that refused to escape by abandoning his friend.

The next hour was a hard repetition of the gully riding, but it was on the highlands where there was snow, and when again the pack was split, we strained every power and succeeded in keeping them on the big "five-fifty track," that already was wearing for me the glamour of romance.

Evidently the Dogs preferred either of the others, but we got them going at last. Another half hour's hard work and far ahead, as I rose to a broad flat plain, I had my first glimpse of the Big Black Wolf of Sentinel Butte.

"Hurrah! Badlands Billy! Hurrah! Badlands Billy!" I shouted in salute, and the others took up the cry.

We were on his track at last, thanks to himself. The Dogs joined in with a louder baying, the Greyhounds yelped and made straight for him, and the Horses sniffed and sprang more gamely as they caught the thrill. The only silent one was the black-maned Wolf, and as I marked his size and power, and above all his long and massive jaws, I knew why the Dogs preferred some other trail.

With head and tail low he was bounding over the snow. His tongue was lolling long; plainly he was hard pressed. The wolvers' hands flew to their revolvers, though he was three hundred yards ahead; they were out for blood, not sport. But an instant later he had sunk from view in the nearest sheltered cañon.

Now which way would he go, up or down the cañon? Up was toward his mountain, down was better cover. King and I thought "up," so pressed westward along the ridge. But the others rode eastward, watching for a chance to shoot.

Soon we had ridden out of hearing. We were wrong—the Wolf had gone down, but we heard no shooting. The cañon was crossable here; we reached the other side and then turned back at a gallop, scanning the snow for a trail, the hills for a moving form, or the wind of a sound of life.

"Squeak, squeak," went our saddle leathers, "puff—puff" our Horses, and their feet "ka-ka-lump, ka-ka-lump."

10

WHEN BILLY WENT BACK TO HIS MOUNTAIN

We were back opposite to where the Wolf had plunged, but saw no sign. We rode at an easy gallop, on eastward a mile, and still on, when King gasped out, "Look at that!" A dark spot was moving on the snow ahead. We put on speed. Another dark spot appeared, and another, but they were not going fast. In five minutes we were near them, to find—three of our own Greyhounds. The had lost sight of the game, and with that their interest waned. Now they were seeking us. We saw nothing there of the chase or of the other hunters. But hastening to the next ridge we stumbled on the trail we sought and followed as hard as though in view. Another cañon came in our path, and as we rode and looked for a place to cross, a wild din of Hounds came from its bushy depth. The clamor grew and passed up the middle.

We raced along the rim, hoping to see the game. The Dogs appeared near the farther side, not in a pack, but a long, straggling line. In five minutes more they rose to the edge, and ahead of them was the great Black Wolf. He was loping as before, head and tail low. Power was plain in every limb, and double power in his jaws and neck, but I thought his bounds were shorter now, and that they had lost their spring. The Dogs slowly reached the upper level, and sighting him they broke into a feeble cry; they, too, were nearly spent. The Greyhounds saw the chase, and leaving us they scrambled down the cañon and up the other side at impetuous speed that would surely break them down, while we rode, vainly seeking means of crossing.

How the wolver raved to see the pack lead off in the climax of the chase, and himself held up behind. But he rode and wrathed and still rode, up to where the cañon dwindled— rough land and a hard ride. As we neared the great flat mountain, the feeble cry of the pack was heard again from the south, then toward the high Butte's side, and just a trifle louder now. We reined in on a hillock and scanned the snow. A moving speck appeared, then others, not bunched, but in a straggling train, and at times there was a far faint cry. They were headed toward us, coming on, yes! coming, but so slowly, for not one was really running now. There was the grim old Cow-killer limping over the ground, and far behind a Greyhound, and another, and farther still, the other Dogs in order of their speed, slowly, gamely, dragging themselves on that pursuit. Many hours of hardest toil had done their work. The Wolf had vainly sought to fling them off. Now was his hour of doom, for he was spent; they still had some reserve. Straight to us for a time they came, skirting the base of the mountain, crawling.

We could not cross to join them, so held our breath and gazed with ravenous eyes. They were nearer now, the wind brought feeble notes from the Hounds. The big Wolf turned to the steep ascent, up a well-known trail, it seemed, for he made no slip. My heart went with him, for he had come back to rescue his friend, and a momentary thrill of pity came over us both, as we saw him glance around and drag himself up the sloping way, to die on his mountain. There was no escape for him, beset by fifteen Dogs with men to back them. He was not walking, but tottering upward; the Dogs behind in line, were now doing a little better, were nearing him. We could hear them gasping; we scarcely heard them bay—they had no breath for that; upward the grim procession went, circling a spur of the Butte and along a ledge that climbed and narrowed, then dropped for a few yards to a shelf that reared above the cañon. The foremost Dogs were closing, fearless of a foe so nearly spent.

Here in the narrowest place, where one wrong step meant death, the great Wolf turned and faced them. With forefeet braced, with head low and tail a little raised, his dusky mane a-bristling, his glittering tusks laid bare, but uttering no sound that we could hear, he faced the crew. His legs were weak with toil, but his neck, his jaws, and his heart were strong, and—now all you who love the Dogs had better close the book—on—up and down—fifteen to one, they came, the swiftest first, and how it was done, the eye could scarcely see, but even as a stream of water pours on a rock to be splashed in broken jets aside, that stream of Dogs came pouring down the path, in single file perforce, and Duskymane received them as they come. A feeble spring, a counter-lunge, a gash, and "Fango's down," has lost his foothold and is gone. Dander and Coalie close and try to clinch; a rush, a heave, and they are fallen from that narrow path. Blue-spot then, backed by mighty Oscar and fearless Tige—but the Wolf is next the rock and the flash of combat clears to show him there alone, the big Dogs gone; the rest close in, the hindmost force the foremost on—down—to their death. Slash, chop and heave, from the swiftest to the biggest, to the last, down—down— he sent them whirling from the ledge to the gaping gulch below, where rocks and snags of trunks were sharp to do their work.

In fifty seconds it was done. The rock had splashed the stream aside—the Penroof pack was all wiped out; and Badlands Billy stood there, alone again on his mountain.

A moment he waited to look for more to come. There were no more, the pack was dead; but waiting he got his breath, then raising his voice for the first time in that fatal scene, he feebly gave a long yell of triumph, and scaling the next low bank, was screened from view in a cañon of Sentinel Butte.

We stared like men of stone. The guns in our hands were forgotten. It was all so quick, so final. We made no move till

the Wolf was gone. It was not far to the place: we went on foot
to see if any had escaped. Not one was left alive. We could do
nothing—we could say nothing.

11

THE HOWL AT SUNSET

A week later we were riding the upper trail back of the
Chimney Pot, King and I. "The old man is pretty sick of it,"
he said. "He'd sell out if he could. He don't know what's the
next move."

The sun went down beyond Sentinel Butte. It was dusk as
we reached the turn that led to Dumont's place, and a deep-
toned rolling howl came from the river flat below, followed
by a number of higher-pitched howls in answering chorus. We
could see nothing, but we listened hard. The song was repeated, the hunting-cry of the Wolves. It faded, the night was
stirred by another, the sharp bark and the short howl, the
signal "close in"; a bellow came up, very short, for it was cut
short.

And King as he touched his Horse said grimly: "That's
him, he is out with the pack, an' thar goes another Beef."

The Boy and the Lynx

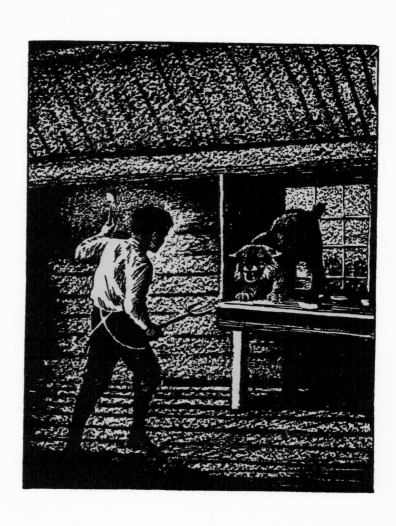

The Boy and the Lynx

1

THE BOY

 E was barely fifteen, a lover of sport and uncommonly keen, even for a beginner. Flocks of Wild Pigeons had been coming all day across the blue Lake of Caygeonull, and perching in lines on the dead limbs of the great rampikes that stood as monuments of fire, around the little clearing in the forest, they afforded tempting marks; but he followed them for hours in vain. They seemed to know the exact range of the old-fashioned shotgun and rose on noisy wings each time before he was near enough to fire. At length a small flock scattered among the low green trees that grew about the spring, near the log shanty, and taking advantage of the cover, Thorburn went in gently. He caught sight of a single Pigeon close to him, took a long aim and fired. A sharp crack resounded at almost the same time and the bird fell dead. Thorburn rushed to seize the prize just as a tall young man stepped into view and picked it up.

"Hello, Corney! you got my bird!"

"Your burrud! Sure yours flew away thayre. I saw them settle hayer and thought I'd make sure of wan with the rifle."

A careful examination showed that a rifle-ball as well as a charge of shot had struck the Pigeon. The gunners had fired on the same bird. Both enjoyed the joke, though it had its serious side, for food as well as ammunition was scarce in that backwoods home.

Corney, a superb specimen of a six-foot Irish-Canadian in early manhood, now led away to the log shanty where the very scarcity of luxuries and the roughness of their lives were sources of merriment. For the Colts, though born and bred in the backwoods of Canada, had lost nothing of the spirit that makes the Irish blood a world-wide synonym of heartiness and wit.

Corney was the eldest son of a large family. The old folks lived at Petersay, twenty-five miles to the southward. He had taken up a "claim" to carve his own home out of the woods at Fenebonk, and his grown sisters, Margat, staid and reliable, and Loo, bright and witty, were keeping house for him. Thorburn Alder was visiting them. He had just recovered from a severe illness and had been sent to rough it in the woods in hope of winning some of the vigor of his hosts. Their home was of unhewn logs, unfloored, and roofed with sods, which bore a luxuriant crop of grass and weeds. The primitive woods around were broken in two places: one where the roughest of roads led southward to Petersay; the other where the sparkling lake rolled on a pebbly shore and gave a glimpse of their nearest neighbor's house—four miles across the water.

Their daily round had little change. Corney was up at daybreak to light the fire, call his sisters, and feed the horses while they prepared breakfast. At six the meal was over and Corney went to his work. At noon, which Margat knew by the shadow of a certain rampike falling on the spring, a clear notification to draw fresh water for the table, Loo would hang a white rag on a pole, and Corney, seeing the signal, would return from summer fallow or hay-field, grimy, swarthy, and ruddy, a picture of manly vigor and honest toil. Thor might be away all day, but at night, when they again assembled at the table, he would come from lake or distant ridge and eat a supper like the dinner and breakfast, for meals as well as days were exact repeats: pork, bread, potatoes, and tea, with occasionally eggs supplied by a dozen hens around the little log stable, with, rarely, a variation of wild meat, for Thor was not a hunter and Corney had little time for anything but the farm.

2

THE LYNX

A huge four-foot basswood had gone the way of all trees. Death had been generous—had sent the three warnings: it was the biggest of its kind, its children were grown up, it was hollow. The wintry blast that sent it down had broken it across and revealed a great hole where should have been its heart. A long wooden cavern in the middle of a sunny opening, it now lay, and presented an ideal home for a Lynx when she sought a sheltered nesting-place for her coming brood.

Old was she and gaunt, for this was a year of hard times for the Lynxes. A Rabbit plague the autumn before had swept away their main support; a winter of deep snow and sudden crusts had killed off nearly all the Partridges; a long wet spring had destroyed the few growing coveys and had kept the ponds and streams so full that Fish and Frogs were safe from their armed paws, and this mother Lynx fared no better than her kind.

The little ones—half starved before they came—were a double drain, for they took the time she might have spent in hunting.

The Northern Hare is the favorite food of the Lynx, and in some years she could have killed fifty in one day, but never one did she see this season. The plague had done its work too well.

One day she caught a Red-squirrel which had run into a hollow log that proved a trap. Another day a fetid Blacksnake was her only food. A day was missed, and the little ones whined piteously for their natural food and failing drink. One day she saw a large black animal of unpleasant but familiar smell. Swiftly and silently she sprang to make attack. She struck it once on the nose, but the Porcupine doubled his head under, his tail flew up, and the mother Lynx was speared in a dozen places with the little stinging javelins. She drew them all with her teeth, for she had "learned Porcupine" years before, and only the hard push of want would have made her strike one now.

A Frog was all she caught that day. On the next, as she ranged the farthest woods in a long, hard hunt, she heard a singular calling voice. It was new to her. She approached it cautiously, up wind, got many new odors and some more strange sounds in coming. The loud, clear, rolling call was repeated as the mother Lynx came to an opening in the forest. In the middle of it were two enormous muskrat or beaverhouses, far bigger than the biggest she ever before had seen. They were made partly of logs and situated, not in a pond, but on a dry knoll. Walking about them were a number of Partridges, that is, birds like Partridges, only larger and of various colors, red, yellow, and white.

She quivered with the excitement that in a man would have been called buck-fever. Food—food—abundance of food, and the old huntress sank to earth. Her breast was on the ground, her elbows above her back, as she made stalk, her shrewdest, subtlest stalk; one of those Partridges she must have at any price; no trick now must go untried, no error in this hunt; if it took hours—all day—she must approach with certainty to win before the quarry took to flight.

Only a few bounds it was from wood shelter to the great rat-house, but she was an hour in crawling that small space. From stump to brush, from log to bunch of grass she sneaked, a flattened form, and the Partridges saw her not. They fed about, the biggest uttering the ringing call that first had fallen on her ear. Once they seemed to sense their peril, but a long await dispelled the fear. Now they were almost in reach, and she trembled with all the eagerness of the hunting heart and the hungry maw. Her eye centered on a white one not quite the nearest, but the color seemed to hold her gaze.

There was an open space around the rat-house; outside that were tall weeds, and stumps were scattered everywhere. The white bird wandered behind these weeds, the red one of the loud voice flew to the top of the rat-mound and sang as before. The mother Lynx sank lower yet. It seemed an alarm note; but no, the white one still was there; she could see its feathers gleaming through the weeds. An open space now lay about. The huntress, flattened like an empty skin, trailed slow and silent on the ground behind a log no thicker than her neck; if she could reach that tuft of brush she could get unseen to the weeds and then would be near enough to spring. She could smell them now—the rich and potent smell of life, of flesh and blood, that set her limbs a-tingle and her eyes a-glow.

The Partridges still scratched and fed; another flew to the high top, but the white one remained. Five more slow-gliding, silent steps, and the Lynx was behind the weeds, the white bird shining through; she gauged the distance, tried the footing, swung her hind legs to clear some fallen brush, then *leaped* direct with all her force, and the white one never knew the death it died, for the fateful gray shadow dropped, the swift and deadly did their work, and before the other birds could realize the foe or fly, the Lynx was gone, with the white bird squirming in her jaws.

Uttering an unnecessary growl of inborn ferocity and joy she bounded into the forest, and bee-like sped for home. The last quiver had gone from the warm body of the victim when she heard the sound of heavy feet ahead. She leaped on a log. The wings of her prey were muffling her eyes, so she laid the bird down and held it safely with one paw. The sound drew nearer, the bushes bent, and a Boy stepped into view. The old Lynx knew and hated his kind. She had watched them at night, had followed them, had been hunted and hurt by them. For a moment they stood face to face. The huntress growled a warning that was also a challenge and a defiance, picked up the bird and bounded from the log into the sheltering bushes. It was a mile or two to the den, but she stayed not to eat till the sunlit opening and the big basswood came to view; then a low "prr—prr" called forth the little ones to revel with their mother in a plenteous meal of the choicest food.

3

THE HOME OF THE LYNX

At first Thor, being town-bred, was timid about venturing into the woods beyond the sound of Corney's axe; but day by day he went farther, guiding himself, not by unreliable moss on trees, but by sun, compass, and landscape features. His purpose was to learn about the wild animals rather than to kill them; but the naturalist is close kin to the sportsman, and the gun was his constant companion. In the clearing, the only animal of any size was a fat Woodchuck; it had a hole under a stump some hundred yards from the shanty. On sunny mornings it used to lie basking on the stump, but eternal vigilance is the price of every good thing in the woods. The Woodchuck was always alert and Thor tried in vain to shoot or even to trap him.

"Hyar," said Corney one morning, "time we had some fresh meat." He took down his rifle, an old-fashioned brass-mounted small-bore, and loading with care that showed the true rifle-man, he steadied the weapon against the door-jamb and fired. The Woodchuck fell backward and lay still. Thor raced to the place and returned in triumph with the animal, shouting: "Plumb through the head—one hundred and twenty yards."

Corney controlled the gratified smile that wrestled with the corners of his mouth, but his bright eyes shone a trifle brighter for the moment.

It was no mere killing for killing's sake, for the Woodchuck was spreading a belt of destruction in the crop around his den. Its flesh supplied the family with more than one good meal and Corney showed Thor how to use the skin. First the pelt was wrapped in hardwood ashes for twenty-four hours. This brought the hair off. Then the skin was soaked for three days in soft soap and worked by hand, as it dried, till it came out a white strong leather.

Thor's wanderings extended farther in search of the things which always came as surprises however much he was looking for them. Many days were blanks and others would be crowded with incidents, for unexpectedness is above all the peculiar feature of hunting, and its lasting charm. One day he had gone far beyond the ridge in a new direction and passed through an open glade where lay the broken trunk of a huge basswood. The size impressed it on his memory. He swung past the glade to make for the lake, a mile to the west, and twenty minutes later he started back as his eye rested on a huge black animal in the crotch of a hemlock, some thirty feet from the ground. A Bear! At last, this was the test of nerve he had half expected all summer; had been wondering how that mystery "himself" would act under this very trial. He stood still; his right hand dived into his pocket and, bringing out three or four buckshot, which he carried for emergency, he dropped them on top of the birdshot already in the gun, then ramed a wad to hold them down.

The Bear had not moved and the boy could not see its head, but now he studied it carefully. It was not such a large one— no, it was a small one, yes, very small—a cub. A cub! That meant a mother Bear at hand, and Thor looked about with some fear, but seeing no signs of any except the little one, he levelled the gun and fired.

Then to his surprise down crashed the animal quite dead; it was not a Bear, but a large Porcupine. As it lay there he examined it with wonder and regret, for he had no wish to kill such a harmless creature. On its grotesque face he found two or three long scratches which proved that he had not been its only enemy. As he turned away he noticed some blood on his trousers, then saw that his left hand was bleeding. He had wounded himself quite severely on the quills of the animal without knowing it. He was sorry to leave the specimen there, and Loo, when she learned of it, said it was a shame not to skin it when she "needed a fur-lined cape for the winter."

On another day Thor had gone without a gun, as he meant only to gather some curious plants he had seen. They were close to the clearing; he knew the place by a fallen elm. As he came to it he heard a peculiar sound. Then on the log his eye caught two moving things. He lifted a bough and got a clear view. They were the head and tail of an enormous Lynx. It had seen him and was glaring and grumbling; and under its foot on the log was a white bird that a second glance showed to be one of their own precious hens. How fierce and cruel the brute looked! How Thor hated it! and fairly gnashed his teeth with disgust that now, when his greatest chance was come, he for once was without his gun. He was in not a little fear, too, and stood wondering what to do. The Lynx growled louder; its stumpy tail twitched viciously for a minute, then it picked up its victim, and leaping from the log was lost to view.

As it was a very rainy summer, the ground was soft every-where, and the young hunter was led to follow tracks that would have defied an expert in dryer times. One day he came on piglike footprints in the woods. He followed them with little difficulty, for they were new, and a heavy rain two hours before had washed out all other trails. After about half a mile they led him to an open ravine, and as he reached its brow he saw across it a flash of white; then his keen young eyes made out the forms of a Deer and a spotted Fawn gazing at him curiously. Though on their trail he was not a little startled. He gazed at them open-mouthed. The mother turned and raised the danger flag, her white tail, and bounded lightly away, to be followed by the youngster, clearing low trunks with an effortless leap, or bending down with catlike suppleness when they came to a log upraised so that they might pass below.

He never again got a chance to shoot at them, though more than once he saw the same two tracks, or believed they were the same, as for some cause never yet explained, Deer were scarcer in that unbroken forest than they were in later years when clearings spread around.

He never again saw *them;* but he saw the mother once—he thought it was the same—she was searching the woods with her nose, trying the ground for trails; she was nervous and anxious, evidently seeking. Thor remembered a trick that Corney had told him. He gently stooped, took up a broad blade of grass, laid it between the edges of his thumbs, then blowing through this simple squeaker he made a short, shrill bleat, a fair imitation of a Fawn's cry for the mother, and the Deer, though a long way off, came bounding toward him. He snatched his gun, meaning to kill her, but the movement caught her eye. She stopped. Her mane bristled a little; she sniffed and looked inquiringly at him. Her big soft eyes touched his heart, held back his hand; she took a cautious step nearer, got a full whiff of her mortal enemy, bounded behind a big tree and away before his merciful impulse was gone. "Poor thing," said Thor, "I believe she has lost her little one."

Yet once more the Boy met a Lynx in the woods. Half an hour after seeing the lonely Deer he crossed the long ridge that lay some miles north of the shanty. He had passed the glade where the great basswood lay when a creature like a big bob-tailed Kitten appeared and looked innocently at him. His gun went up, as usual, but the Kitten merely cocked its head on one side and fearlessly surveyed him. Then a second one that he had not noticed before began to play with the first, pawing at its tail and inviting its brother to tussle.

Thor's first thought to shoot was stayed as he watched their gambols, but the remembrance of his feud with their race came back. He had almost raised the gun when a fierce rumble close at hand gave him a start, and there, not ten feet from him, stood the old one, looking big and fierce as a Tigress. It was surely folly to shoot at the young ones now. The boy nervously dropped some buckshot on the charge while the snarling growl rose and fell, but before he was ready to shoot at her the old one had picked up something that was by her feet; the boy got a glimpse of rich brown with white spots—the limp form of a newly killed Fawn. Then she passed out of sight. The Kittens followed, and he saw her no more until the time when, life against life, they were weighed in the balance together.

4

THE TERROR OF THE WOODS

Six weeks had passed in daily routine when one day the young giant seemed unusually quiet as he went about. His handsome face was very sober and he sang not at all that morning.

He and Thor slept on a hay-bunk in one corner of the main room, and that night the Boy awakened more than once to hear his companion groaning and tossing in his sleep.

Corney arose as usual in the morning and fed the horses, but lay down again while the sisters got breakfast. He roused himself by an effort and went back to work, but came home early. He was trembling from head to foot. It was hot summer weather, but he could not be kept warm. After several hours a reaction set in and Corney was in a high fever. The family knew well now that he had the dreaded chills and fever of the backwoods. Margat went out and gathered a lapful of pipsissewa to make tea, of which Corney was encouraged to drink copiously.

But in spite of all their herbs and nursing the young man got worse. At the end of ten days he was greatly reduced in flesh and incapable of work, so on one of the "well days" that are usual in the course of the disease he said:

"Say, gurruls, I can't stand it no longer. Guess I better go home. I'm well enough to drive to-day, for a while anyway; if I'm took down I'll lay in the wagon, and the horses will fetch me home. Mother'll have me all right in a week or so. If you run out of grub before I come back take the canoe to Ellerton's."

So the girls harnessed the horses; the wagon was partly filled with hay, and Corney, weak and white-faced, drove away on the long rough road, and left them feeling much as though they were on a desert island and their only boat had been taken from them.

Half a week had scarcely gone before all three of them, Mar-

PIPSISSEWA

gat, Loo, and Thor, were taken down with a yet more virulent form of chills and fever.

Corney had had every other a "well day," but with these three there were no "well days" and the house became an abode of misery.

Seven days passed, and now Margat could not leave her bed and Loo was barely able to walk around the house. She was a brave girl with a fund of drollery which did much toward keeping up all their spirits, but her merriest jokes fell ghastly from her wan, pinched face. Thor, though weak and ill, was the strongest and did for the others, cooking and serving each day a simple meal, for they could eat very little, fortunately, perhaps, as there was very little, and Corney could not return for another week.

Soon Thor was the only one able to rise, and one morning when he dragged himself to cut the little usual slice of their treasured bacon he found, to his horror, that the whole piece was gone. It had been stolen, doubtless by some wild animal, from the little box on the shady side of the house, where it was kept safe from flies. Now they were down to flour and tea. He was in despair, when his eye lighted on the Chickens about the stable; but what's the use? In his feeble state he might as well try to catch a Deer or a Hawk. Suddenly he remembered his gun and very soon was preparing a fat Hen for the pot. He boiled it whole as the easiest way to cook it, and the broth was the first really tempting food they had had for some time.

They kept alive for three wretched days on that Chicken, and when it was finished Thor again took down his gun—it seemed a much heavier gun now. He crawled to the barn, but he was so weak and shaky that he missed several times before he brought down a fowl. Corney had taken the rifle away with him and three charges of gun ammunition were all that now remained.

Thor was surprised to see how few Hens there were now, only three or four. There used to be over a dozen. Three days later he made another raid. He saw but one Hen and he used up his last ammunition to get that.

His daily routine now was a monotony of horror. In the morning, which was his "well time," he prepared a little food for the household and got ready for the night of raging fever by putting a bucket of water on a block at the head of each bunk. About one o'clock, with fearful regularity, the chills would come on, with trembling from head to foot and chattering teeth, and cold, cold, within and without. Nothing seemed to give any warmth—fire seemed to have lost its power. There was nothing to do but to lie and shake and suffer all the slow torture of freezing to death and shaking to pieces. For six hours it would keep up, and to the torture, nausea lent its horrid aid throughout; then about seven or eight o'clock in the evening a change would come; a burning fever set in; no ice could have seemed cool to him then; water—water—was all he craved, and drank and drank until three or four in the morning, when the fever would abate, and a sleep of total exhaustion followed.

"If you run out of food take the canoe to Ellerton's," was the brother's last word. Who was to take the canoe?

There was but half a Chicken now between them and starvation, and no sign of Corney.

For three interminable weeks the deadly program dragged along. It went on the same yet worse, as the sufferers grew weaker—a few days more and the Boy also would be unable to leave his couch. Then what?

Despair was on the house and the silent cry of each was, "Oh, God! will Corney never come?"

5

THE HOME OF THE BOY

On the day of that last Chicken, Thor was all morning carrying water enough for the coming three fevers. The chill attacked him sooner than it was due and his fever was worse than ever before.

He drank deeply and often from the bucket at his head. He had filled it, and it was nearly emptied when about two in the morning the fever left him and he fell asleep.

In the gray dawn he was awakened by a curious sound not far away—a splashing of water. He turned his head to see two glaring eyes within a foot of his face—a great Beast lapping the water in the bucket by his bed.

Thor gazed in horror for a moment, then closed his eyes, sure that he was dreaming, certain that this was a nightmare of India with a Tiger by his couch; but the lapping continued. He looked up; yes, it still was there. He tried to find his voice but uttered only a gurgle. The great furry head quivered, a sniff came from below the shining eyeballs, and the creature, whatever it was, dropped to its front feet and went across the hut under the table. Thor was fully awake now; he rose slowly on his elbow and feebly shouted "Sssh-hi," at which the shining eyes reappeared under the table and the gray form came forth. Calmly it walked across the ground and glided under the lowest log at a place where an old potato-pit left an opening and disappeared.

What was it? The sick boy hardly knew—some savage Beast of prey, undoubtedly. He was totally unnerved. He shook with fear and a sense of helplessness, and the night passed in fitful sleep and sudden starts awake to search the gloom again for those fearful eyes and the great gray gliding form. In the morning he did not know whether it were not all a delirium, yet he made a feeble effort to close the old cellar hole with some firewood.

The three had little appetite, but even that they restrained since now they were down to part of a Chicken, and Corney, evidently he supposed they had been to Ellerton's and got all the food they needed.

Again that night, when the fever left him weak and dozing, Thor was awakened by a noise in the room, a sound of crunching bones. He looked around to see dimly outlined against the little window, the form of a large animal on the table. Thor shouted; he tried to hurl his boot at the intruder. It leaped lightly to the ground and passed out of the hole, again wide open.

It was no dream this time, he knew, and the women knew it, too; not only had they heard the creature, but the Chicken, the last of their food, was wholly gone.

Poor Thor barely left his couch that day. It needed all the querulous complaints of the sick women to drive him forth. Down by the spring he found a few berries and divided them with the others. He made his usual preparations for the chills and the thirst, but he added this—by the side of his couch he put an old fish-spear—the only weapon he could find, now the gun was useless—a pine-root candle and some matches. He knew the Beast was coming back again—was coming hungry. It would find no food; what more natural, he thought, than take the living prey lying there so helpless? And a vision came of the limp brown form of the little Fawn, borne off in those same cruel jaws.

Once again he barricaded the hole with firewood, and the night passed as usual, but without any fierce visitor. Their food that day was flour and water, and to cook it Thor was forced to use some of his barricade. Loo attempted some feeble joke, guessed she was light enough to fly now and tried to rise, but she got no farther than the edge of the bunk. The same preparations were made, and the night wore on, but early in the morning, Thor was again awakened rudely by the sound of lapping water by his bed, and there, as before, were the glowing eyeballs, the great head, the gray form relieved by the dim light from the dawning window.

Thor put all his strength into what was meant for a bold shout, but it was merely a feeble screech. He rose slowly and called out: "Loo, Margat! The Lynx—here's the Lynx again!"

"May God help ye, for we can't," was the answer.

"Sssh-hi!" Thor tried again to drive the Beast away. It leaped on to the table by the window and stood up growling under the useless gun. Thor thought it was going to leap through the glass as it faced the window a moment; but it turned and glared toward the Boy, for he could see both eyes shining. He rose slowly to the side of his bunk and he prayed for help, for he felt it was kill or be killed. He struck a match and lighted his pine-root candle, held that in his left hand and in his right took the old fish-spear, meaning to fight, but he was so weak he had to use the fish-spear as a crutch. The great Beast stood on the table still, but was crouching a little as though for a spring. Its eyes glowed red in the torchlight. Its short tail was switching from side to side and its growling took a higher pitch. Thor's knees were smiting together, but he levelled the spear and made a feeble lunge toward the brute. It sprang at the same moment, not at him, as he first thought —the torch and the boy's bold front had had effect—it went over his head to drop on the ground beyond and at once to slink under the bunk.

This was only a temporary repulse. Thor set the torch on a ledge of the logs, then took the spear in both hands. He was fighting for his life, and he knew it. He heard the voices of the women feebly praying. He saw only the glowing eyes under the bed and heard the growling in higher pitch as the Beast was nearing action. He steadied himself by a great effort and plunged the spear with all the force he could give it.

It struck something softer than the logs: a hideous snarl came forth. The boy threw all his weight on the weapon; the Beast was struggling to get at him; he felt its teeth and claws grating on the handle, and in spite of himself it was coming on; its powerful arms and claws were reaching for him now; he could not hold out long. He put on all his force, just a little more it was than before; the Beast lurched, there was a growling, a crack, and a sudden.yielding; the rotten old spear-head had broken off, the Beast sprang out—at him— past him—never touched him, but across through the hole and away, to be seen no more.

Thor fell on the bed and lost all consciousness.

He lay there he knew not how long, but was awakened in broad daylight by a loud, cheery voice:

"Hello! Hello!—are ye all dead? Loo! Thor! Margat!"

He had no strength to answer, but there was a trampling of horses outside, a heavy step, the door was forced open, and

in strode Corney, handsome and hearty as ever. But what a
flash of horror and pain came over his face on entering the
silent shanty!

"Dead?" he gasped. "Who's dead—where are you? Thor?"
Then, "Who is it? Loo? Margat?"

"Corney—Corney," came feebly from the bunk. "They're
in there. They're awful sick. We have nothing to eat."

"Oh, what a fool I be!" said Corney again and again. "I
made sure ye'd go to Ellerton's and get all ye wanted."

"We had no chance, Corney; we were all three brought
down at once, right after you left. Then the Lynx came and
cleared up the Hens, and all in the house, too."

"Well, ye got even with her," and Corney pointed to the
trail of blood across the mud floor and out under the logs.

Good food, nursing, and medicine restored them all.

A month or two later, when the women wanted a new
leaching-barrel, Thor said: "I know where there is a hollow
basswood as big as a hogshead."

He and Corney went to the place, and when they cut off
what they needed, they found in the far end of it the dried-up
bodies of two little Lynxes with that of the mother, and in
the side of the old one was the head of a fish-spear broken
from the handle.

Little Warhorse

THE HISTORY OF A JACK-RABBIT

Little Warhorse

1

THE Little Warhorse knew practically all the Dogs in town. First, there was a very large brown Dog that had pursued him many times, a Dog that he always got rid of by slipping through a hole in a board fence. Second, there was a small active Dog that could follow through that hole, and him he baffled by leaping a twenty-foot irrigation ditch that had steep sides and a swift current. The Dog could not make this leap. It was "sure medicine" for that foe, and the boys still call the place "Old Jacky's Jump." But there was a Greyhound that could leap better than the Jack, and when he could not follow through a fence, he jumped over it. He tried the Warhorse's mettle more than once, and Jacky only saved himself by his quick dodging, till they got to an Osage hedge, and here the Greyhound had to give it up. Besides these, there was in town a rabble of big and little Dogs that were troublesome, but easily left behind in the open.

In the country there was a Dog at each farm-house, but

only one that the Warhorse really feared; that was a long-legged, fierce, black Dog, a brute so swift and pertinacious that he had several times forced the Warhorse almost to the last extremity.

For the town Cats he cared little; only once or twice had he been threatened by them. A huge Tom-cat flushed with many victories came crawling up to where he fed one moonlight night. Jack Warhorse saw the black creature with the glowing eyes, and a moment before the final rush, he faced it, raised up on his haunches,—his hind legs,—at full length on his toes,—with his broad ears towering up yet six inches higher; then letting out a loud *churrr-churrr,* his best attempt at a roar, he sprang five feet forward and landed on the Cat's head, driving in his sharp hind nails, and the old Tom fled in terror from the weird two-legged giant. This trick he had tried several times with success, but twice it turned out a sad failure: once, when the Cat proved to be a mother whose Kittens were near; then Jack Warhorse had to flee for his life; and the other time was when he made the mistake of landing hard on a Skunk.

But the Greyhound was the dangerous enemy, and in him the Warhorse might have found his fate, but for a curious adventure with a happy ending for Jack.

He fed by night; there were fewer enemies about then, and it was easier to hide; but one day at dawn in winter he had lingered long at an alfalfa stack and was crossing the open snow toward his favorite form, when, as ill-luck would have it, he met the Greyhound prowling outside the town. With open snow and growing daylight there was no chance to hide, nothing but a run in the open with soft snow that hindered the Jack more than it did the Hound.

Off they went—superb runners in fine fettle. How they

skimmed across the snow, raising it in little *puff—puff—puffs,*
each time their nimble feet went down. This way and that,
swerving and dodging, went the chase. Everything favored
the Dog,—his empty stomach, the cold weather, the soft
snow,—while the Rabbit was handicapped by his heavy meal
of alfalfa. But his feet went *puff—puff* so fast that a dozen
of the little snow-jets were in view at once. The chase continued in the open; no friendly hedge was near, and every
attempt to reach a fence was cleverly stopped by the Hound.
Jack's ears were losing their bold up-cock, a sure sign of failing heart or wind, when all at once these flags went stiffly
up, as under sudden renewal of strength. The Warhorse put
forth all his power, not to reach the hedge to the north, but
over the open prairie eastward. The Greyhound followed,
and within fifty yards the Jack dodged to foil his fierce pursuer; but on the next tack he was on his eastern course again,
and so tacking and dodging, he kept the line direct for the
next farm-house, where was a very high board fence with a
henhole, and where also there dwelt his other hated enemy,
the big black Dog. An outer hedge delayed the Greyhound for
a moment and gave Jack time to dash through the hen-hole
into the yard, where he hid to one side. The Greyhound
rushed around to the low gate, leaped over that among the
Hens, and as they fled cackling and fluttering, some Lambs
bleated loudly. Their natural guardian, the big black Dog,
ran to the rescue, and Warhorse slipped out again by the
hole at which he had entered. Horrible sounds of Dog hate
and fury were heard behind him in the hen-yard, and soon
the shouts of men were added. How it ended he did not
know or seek to learn, but it was remarkable that he never
afterward was troubled by the swift Greyhound that formerly
lived in Newchusen.

2

Hard times and easy times had long followed in turn and been taken as matters of course; but recent years in the State of Kaskado had brought to the Jack-rabbits a succession of remarkable ups and downs. In the old days they had their endless fight with Birds and Beasts of Prey, with cold and heat, with pestilence and with flies whose sting bred a loathsome disease, and yet had held their own. But the settling of the country by farmers made many changes.

Dogs and guns arriving in numbers reduced the ranks of Coyotes, Foxes, Wolves, Badgers, and Hawks that preyed on the Jack, so that in a few years the Rabbits were multiplied in great swarms; but now Pestilence broke out and swept them away. Only the strongest—the double-seasoned—remained. For a while a Jack-rabbit was a rarity; but during this time another change came in. The Osage-orange hedges planted everywhere afforded a new refuge, and now the safety of a Jack-rabbit was less often his speed than his wits, and the wise ones, when pursued by a Dog or Coyote, would rush to the nearest hedge through a small hole and escape while the enemy sought for a larger one by which to follow. The Coyotes rose to this and developed the trick of the relay chase. In this one Coyote takes one field, another the next, and if the Rabbit attempts the "hedge-ruse" they work from each side and usually win their prey. The Rabbit remedy for this, is keen eyes to see the second Coyote, avoidance of that field, then good legs to distance the first enemy.

Thus the Jack-rabbits, after being successively numerous, scarce, in myriads, and rare, were now again on the increase, and those which survived, selected by a hundred hard trials, were enabled to flourish where their ancestors could not have outlived a single season.

Their favorite grounds were, not the broad open stretches of the big ranches, but the complicated, much-fenced fields of the farms, where these were so small and close as to be like a big straggling village.

One of these vegetable villages had sprung up around the railway station of Newchusen. The country a mile away was well supplied with Jack-rabbits of the new and selected stock. Among them was a little lady Rabbit called "Bright-eyes," from her leading characteristic as she sat gray in the gray brush. She was a good runner, but was especially successful with the fence-play that baffled the Coyotes. She made her nest out in an open pasture, an untouched tract of the ancient prairie. Here her brood were born and raised. One like herself was bright-eyed, in coat of silver-gray, and partly gifted with her ready wits, but in the other there appeared a rare combination of his mother's gifts with the best that was in the best strain of the new Jack-rabbits of the plains.

This was the one whose adventures we have been following, the one that later on the turf won the name of Little Warhorse and that afterward achieved a world-wide fame.

Ancient tricks of his kind he revived and put to new uses, and ancient enemies he learned to fight with new-found tricks.

When a mere baby he discovered a plan that was worthy of the wisest Rabbit in Kaskado. He was pursued by a horrible little Yellow Dog, and he had tried in vain to get rid of him by dodging among the fields and farms. This is a good play against a Coyote, because the farmers and the Dogs will often help the Jack, without knowing it, by attacking the Coyote. But now the plan did not work at all, for the little Dog managed to keep after him through one fence after another, and Jack Warhorse, not yet full-grown, must less seasoned, was beginning to feel the strain. His ears were no longer up straight, but angling back and at times drooping to a level, as he darted through a very little hole in an Osage hedge, only to find that his nimble enemy had done the same without loss of time. In the middle of the field was a small herd of cattle and with them a calf.

There is in wild animals a curious impulse to trust any stranger when in desperate straits. The foe behind they know means death. There is just a chance, and the only one left, that the stranger may prove friendly; and it was this last desperate chance that drew Jack Warhorse to the Cows.

It is quite sure that the Cows would have stood by in stolid indifference so far as the Rabbit was concerned, but they have a deep-rooted hatred of a Dog, and when they saw the Yellow Cur coming bounding toward them, their tails and noses went up; they sniffed angrily, then closed up ranks, and led by the Cow that owned the Calf, they charged at the Dog, while Jack took refuge under a low thorn-bush. The Dog swerved aside to attack the Calf, at least the old Cow thought he did, and she followed him so fiercely that he barely escaped from that field with his life.

It was a good old plan—one that doubtless came from the days when Buffalo and Coyote played the parts of Cow and Dog. Jack never forgot it, and more than once it saved his life.

In color as well as in power he was a rarity.

Animals are colored in one or other of two general plans: one that matches them with their surroundings and helps them to hide—this is called "protective"; the other that makes them very visible for several purposes—this is called "directive." Jack-rabbits are peculiar in being painted both ways. As they squat in their form in the gray brush or clods, they are soft gray on their ears, head, back, and sides; they match the ground and cannot be seen until close at hand—they are *protectively* colored. But the moment it is clear to the Jack that the approaching foe will find him, he jumps up and dashes away. He throws off all disguise now, the gray seems to disappear; he makes a lightning change, and his ears show snowy white with black tips, the legs are white, his tail is a black spot in a blaze of white. He is a black-and-white Rabbit now. His coloring is all *directive*. How is it done? Very simply. The front side of the ear is gray, the back, black and white. The black tail with its white halo, and the legs, are tucked below. He is sitting on them. The gray mantle is pulled down and enlarged as he sits, but when he jumps up it shrinks somewhat, all his black-and-white marks are now shown, and just as his colors formerly whispered, "I am a clod," they now shout aloud, "I am a Jack-rabbit."

Why should he do this? Why should a timid creature running for his life thus proclaim to all the world his name instead of trying to hide? There must be some good reason. It must pay, or the Rabbit would never have done it. The answer is, if the creature that scared him up was one of his own kind—i.e., this was a false alarm—then at once, by showing his national colors, the mistake is made right. On the other hand, if it be a Coyote, Fox, or Dog, they see at once, this is a Jack-rabbit, and know that it would be a waste of time for them to pursue him. They say in effect, "This is a Jack-rabbit, and I cannot catch a Jack in open race." They give it up, and that, of course, saves the Jack a great deal of unnecessary running and worry. The black-and-white spots are the national uniform and flag of the Jacks. In poor specimens they are apt to be dull, but in the finest specimens they are not only larger, but brighter than usual, and the Little Warhorse, gray when he sat in his form, blazed like charcoal and snow when he flung his defiance to the Fox and buff Coyote, and danced with little effort before them, first a black-and-white Jack, then a little white spot and last a speck of thistledown, before the distance swallowed him.

Many of the farmers' Dogs had learned the lesson: "A grayish Rabbit you may catch, but a very black-and-white one is hopeless." They might, indeed, follow for a time, but that was merely for the fun of a chivvy, and his growing power often led Warhorse to seek the chase for the sake of a little excitement, and to take hazards that others less gifted were most careful to avoid.

Jack, like all other wild animals, had a certain range or country which was home to him, and outside of this he rarely strayed. It was about three miles across, extending easterly from the center of the village. Scattered through this he had a number of "forms," or "beds" as they are locally called. These were mere hollows situated under a sheltering bush or bunch of grass, without lining excepting the accidental grass and in-blown leaves. But comfort was not forgotten. Some of them were for hot weather; they faced the north, were scarcely sunk, were little more than shady places. Some for the cold weather were deep hollows with southern exposure, and others for the wet were well roofed with herbage and faced the west. In one or other of these he spent the day, and at night he went forth to feed with his kind, sporting and romping on the moonlight nights like a lot of puppy Dogs, but careful to be gone by sunrise, and safely tucked in a bed that was suited to the weather.

The safest ground for the Jacks was among the farms, where not only Osage hedges, but also the newly arrived barb-wire, made hurdles and hazards in the path of possible enemies. But the finest of the forage is nearer to the village among the truck-farms—the finest of forage and the fiercest of dangers. Some of the dangers of the plains were lacking, but the greater perils of men, guns, Dogs, and impassable fences are much increased. Yet those who knew Warhorse best were not at all surprised to find that he had made a form in the middle of a market-gardener's melon-patch. A score of dangers beset him here, but there was also a score of unusual delights and a score of holes in the fence for times when he had to fly, with at least twoscore of expedients to help him afterward.

3

Newchusen was a typical Western town. Everywhere in it, were to be seen strenuous efforts at uglification, crowned with unmeasured success. The streets were straight level lanes without curves or beauty-spots. The houses were cheap and mean structures of flimsy boards and tar paper, and not even honest in their ugliness, for each of them was pretending to be something better than itself. One had a false front to make it look like two stories, another was of imitation brick, a third pretended to be a marble temple.

But all agreed in being the ugliest things ever used as human dwellings, and in each could be read the owner's secret thought—to stand it for a year or so, then move out somewhere else. The only beauties of the place, and those unintentional, were the long lines of hand-planted shade-trees, uglified as far as possible with whitewashed trunks and croppy heads, but still lovable, growing, living things.

The only building in town with a touch of picturesqueness was the grain elevator. It was not posing as a Greek temple or a Swiss châlet, but simply a strong, rough, honest, grain elevator. At the end of each street was a vista of the prairie, with its farm-houses, windmill pumps, and long lines of Osage-orange hedges. Here at least was something of interest —the gray-green hedges, thick, sturdy, and high, were dotted with their golden mock-oranges, useless fruit, but more welcome here than rain in a desert; for these balls were things of beauty, and swung on their long tough boughs they formed with the soft green leaves a color-chord that pleased the weary eye.

Such a town is a place to get out of, as soon as possible, so thought the traveller who found himself laid over here for two days in late winter. He asked after the sights of the place. A white Muskrat stuffed in a case "down to the saloon"; old Baccy Bullin, who had been scalped by the Indians forty years ago; and a pipe once smoked by Kit Carson, proved unattractive, so he turned toward the prairie, still white with snow.

A mark among the numerous Dog tracks caught his eye: it was the track of a large Jack-rabbit. He asked a passer-by if there were any Rabbits in town.

"No, I reckon not. I never seen none," was the answer. A mill-hand gave the same reply, but a small boy with a bundle of newspapers said: "You bet there is; there's lots of them out there on the prairie, and they come in town a-plenty. Why, there's a big, big feller lives right round Si Kalb's melon-patch—oh, an awful big feller, and just as black and as white as checkers!" and thus he sent the stranger eastward on his walk.

The "big, big, awful big one" was the Little Warhorse

himself. He didn't live in Kalb's melon-patch; he was there
only at odd times. He was not there now; he was in his west-
fronting form or bed, because a raw east wind was setting
in. It was due east of Madison Avenue, and as the stranger
plodded that way the Rabbit watched him. As long as the
man kept the road the Jack was quiet, but the road turned
shortly to the north, and the man by chance left it and came
straight on. Then the Jack saw trouble ahead. The moment
the man left the beaten track, he bounded from his form,
and wheeling, he sailed across the prairie due east.

A Jack-rabbit running from its enemy ordinarily covers
eight or nine feet at a bound, and once in five or six bounds,
it makes an observation hop, leaping not along, but high in
the air, so as to get above all herbage and bushes and take
in the situation. A silly young Jack will make an observation
hop as often as one in four, and so waste a great deal of time.
A clever Jack will make one hop in eight or nine, do for
observation. But Jack Warhorse as he sped, got all the information he needed, in one hop out of a dozen, while ten to
fourteen feet were covered by each of his flying bounds. Yet
another personal peculiarity showed in the trail he left. When
a Cottontail or a Wood-hare runs, his tail is curled up tight
on his back, and does not touch the snow. When a Jack runs,
his tail hangs downward or backward, with the tip curved
or straight, according to the individual; in some, it points
straight down, and so, often leaves a little stroke behind the
foot-marks. The Warhorse's tail of shining black was of unusual length, and at every bound, it left in the snow a long
stroke, so that that alone was almost enough to tell which
Rabbit had made the track.

Now some Rabbits seeing only a man without any Dog
would have felt little fear, but Warhorse, remembering some

former stinging experiences with a far-killer, fled when the foe was seventy-five yards away, and skimming low, he ran southeast to a fence that ran easterly. Behind this he went like a low-flying Hawk, till a mile away he reached another of his beds; and here, after an observation taken as he stood on his heels, he settled again to rest.

But not for long. In twenty minutes his great megaphone ears, so close to the ground, caught a regular sound—crunch, crunch, crunch—the tramp of a human foot, and he started up to see the man with the shining stick in his hand, now drawing near.

Warhorse bounded out and away for the fence. Never once did he rise to a "spy-hop" till the wire and rails were between him and his foe, an unnecessary precaution as it chanced, for the man was watching the trail and saw nothing of the Rabbit.

Jack skimmed along, keeping low and looking out for other enemies. He knew now that the man was on his track, and the old instinct born of ancestral trouble with Weasels was doubtless what prompted him to do the double trail. He ran in a long, straight course to a distant fence, followed its far side for fifty yards, then doubling back he retraced his trail and ran off in a new direction till he reached another of his dens or forms. He had been out all night and was very ready to rest, now that the sun was ablaze on the snow; but he had hardly got the place a little warmed when the "tramp, tramp, tramp" announced the enemy, and he hurried away.

After a half-a-mile run he stopped on a slight rise and marked the man still following, so he made a series of wonderful quirks in his trail, a succession of blind zigzags that would have puzzled most trailers; then running a hundred yards past a favorite form, he returned to it from the other side, and settled to rest, sure that now the enemy would be finally thrown off the scent.

It was slower than before, but still it came—"tramp, tramp, tramp."

Jack awoke, but sat still. The man tramped by on the trail one hundred yards in front of him, and as he went on, Jack sprang out unseen, realizing that this was an unusual occasion needing a special effort. They had gone in a vast circle around the home range of the Warhorse and now were less than a mile from the farm-house of the black Dog. There was that wonderful board fence with the happily planned hen-hole. It was a place of good memory—here more than once he had won, here especially he had baffled the Greyhound.

These doubtless were the motive thoughts rather than any plan of playing one enemy against another, and Warhorse bounded openly across the snow to the fence of the big black Dog.

The hen-hole was shut, and Warhorse, not a little puzzled, sneaked around to find another, without success, until, around the front, here was the gate wide open, and inside lying on some boards was the big Dog, fast asleep. The Hens were sitting hunched up in the warmest corner of the yard. The house Cat was gingerly picking her way from barn to kitchen, as Warhorse halted in the gateway.

The black form of his pursuer was crawling down the far white prairie slope. Jack hopped quietly into the yard. A long-legged Rooster, that ought to have minded his own business, uttered a loud cackle as he saw the Rabbit hopping near. The Dog lying in the sun raised his head and stood up, and Jack's peril was dire. He squatted low and turned himself into a gray clod. He did it cleverly, but still might have been lost but for the Cat. Unwittingly, unwillingly, she saved him. The black Dog had taken three steps toward the Warhorse, though he did not know the Rabbit was there, and was now blocking the only way of escape from the yard, when the Cat came round the corner of the house, and leaping to a window-ledge brought a flower-pot rolling down. By that single awkward act she disturbed the armed neutrality existing between herself and the Dog. She fled to the barn, and of course a flying foe is all that is needed to send a Dog on the war-path. They passed within thirty feet of the crouching Rabbit. As soon as they were well gone, Jack turned, and without even a "Thank you, Pussy," he fled to the open and away on the hard-beaten road.

The Cat had been rescued by the lady of the house; the Dog was once more sprawling on the boards when the man on Jack's trail arrived. He carried, not a gun, but a stout stick, sometimes called "dog-medicine," and that was all that prevented the Dog from attacking the enemy of his prey.

This seemed to be the end of the trail. The trick, whether planned or not, was a success, and the Rabbit got rid of his troublesome follower.

Next day the stranger made another search for the Jack and found, not himself, but his track. He knew it by its tail-mark, its long leaps and few spy-hops, but with it and running by it was the track of a smaller Rabbit. Here is where they met, here they chased each other in play, for no signs of battle were there to be seen; here they fed or sat together in the sun, there they ambled side by side, and here again they sported in the snow, always together. There was only one conclusion: this was the mating season. This was a pair of Jack-rabbits—the Little Warhorse and his mate.

4

Next summer was a wonderful year for the Jack-rabbits. A foolish law had set a bounty on Hawks and Owls and had caused a general massacre of these feathered policemen. Consequently the Rabbits had multiplied in such numbers that they now were threatening to devastate the country.

The farmers, who were the sufferers from the bounty law, as well as the makers of it, decided on a great Rabbit drive. All the county was invited to come, on a given morning, to the main road north of the county, with the intention of sweeping the whole region up-wind and at length driving the Rabbits into a huge corral of close wire netting. Dogs were barred as unmanageable, and guns as dangerous in a crowd; but every man and boy carried a couple of long sticks and a bag full of stones. Women came on horseback and in buggies; many carried rattles or horns and tins to make a noise. A number of the buggies trailed a string of old cans or tied laths to scrape on the wheel-spokes, and thus add no little to the deafening clatter of the drive. As Rabbits have marvellously sensitive hearing, a noise that is distracting to mankind, is likely to prove bewildering to them.

The weather was right, and at eight in the morning the word to advance was given. The line was about five miles long at first, and there was a man or a boy every thirty or forty yards. The buggies and riders kept perforce almost entirely to the roads; but the beaters were supposed, as a point of honor, to face everything, and keep the front unbroken. The advance was roughly in three sides of a square. Each man made as much noise as he could, and threshed every bush in his path. A number of Rabbits hopped out.

Some made for the lines, to be at once assailed by a shower of stones that laid many of them low. One or two did get through and escaped, but the majority were swept before the drive. At first the number seen was small, but before three miles were covered the Rabbits were running ahead in every direction. After five miles—and that took about three hours—the word for the wings to close in was given. The space between the men was shortened up till they were less than ten feet apart, and the whole drive converged on the corral with its two long guide wings or fences; the end lines joined these wings, and the surround was complete. The drivers marched rapidly now; scores of the Rabbits were killed as they ran too near the beaters. Their bodies strewed the ground, but the swarms seemed to increase; and in the final move, before the victims were cooped up in the corral, the two-acre space surrounded was a whirling throng of skurrying, jumping, bounding Rabbits. Round and round they circled and leaped, looking for a chance to escape; but the inexorable crowd grew thicker as the ring grew steadily smaller, and the whole swarm was forced along the chute into the tight corral, some to squat stupidly in the middle, some to race round the outer wall, some to seek hiding in corners or under each other.

And the Little Warhorse—where was he in all this? The drive had swept him along, and he had been one of the first to enter the corral. But a curious plan of selection had been established. The pen was to be a death-trap for the Rabbits, except the best, the soundest. And many were there that were unsound; those that think of all wild animals as pure and perfect things, would have been shocked to see how many halt, maimed, and diseased there were in that pen of four thousand or five thousand Jack-rabbits.

It was a Roman victory—the rabble of prisoners was to be butchered. The choicest were to be reserved for the arena. The arena? Yes, that is the Coursing Park.

In that corral trap, prepared beforehand for the Rabbits, were a number of small boxes along the wall, a whole series of them, five hundred at least, each large enough to hold one Jack.

In the last rush of driving, the swiftest Jacks got first to the pen. Some were swift and silly; when once inside they rushed wildly round and round. Some were swift and wise; they quickly sought the hiding afforded by the little boxes; all of these were now full. Thus five hundred of the swiftest had been selected, in not by any means an infallible way, but the simplest and readiest. These five hundred were destined to be coursed by Greyhounds. The surging mass of over four thousand were ruthlessly given to slaughter.

Five hundred little boxes with five hundred bright-eyed Jack-rabbits were put on the train that day, and among them was Little Jack Warhorse.

5

Rabbits take their troubles lightly, and it is not to be supposed that any great terror was felt by the boxed Jacks, once the uproar of the massacre was over; and when they reached the Coursing Park near the great city and were turned out one by one, very gently,—yes, gently; the Roman guards were careful of their prisoners, being responsible for them, —the Jacks found little to complain of, a big enclosure with plenty of good food, and no enemies to annoy them.

The very next morning their training began. A score of
hatchways were opened into a much larger field—the Park.
After a number of Jacks had wandered out through these
doors a rabble of boys appeared and drove them back, pur-
suing them noisily until all were again in the smaller field,
called the Haven. A few days of this taught the Jack-rabbits
that when pursued their safety was to get back by one of the
hatches into the Haven.

Now the second lesson began. The whole band were driven
out of a side door into a long lane which led around three
sides of the Park to another enclosure at the far end. This
was the Starting Pen. Its door into the arena—that is, the
Park—was opened, the Rabbits driven forth, and then a mob
of boys and Dogs in hiding, burst forth and pursued them
across the open. The whole army went bobbing and bounding away, some of the younger ones soaring in a spy-hop, as
a matter of habit; but low skimming ahead of them all was
a gorgeous black-and-white one; clean-limbed and bright-
eyed, he had attracted attention in the pen, but now in the
field he led the band with easy lope that put him as far ahead
of them all as they were ahead of the rabble of common Dogs.

"Luk at thot, would ye—but ain't he a Little Warhorse?"
shouted a villainous-looking Irish stable-boy, and thus he was
named. When half-way across the course the Jacks remembered the Haven, and all swept toward it and in like a snow-
cloud over the drifts.

This was the second lesson—to lead straight for the Haven
as soon as driven from the Pen. In a week all had learned
it, and were ready for the great opening meet of the Coursing
Club.

The Little Warhorse was now well known to the grooms
and hangers-on; his colors usually marked him clearly, and

his leadership was in a measure recognized by the long-eared herd that fled with him. He figured more or less with the Dogs in the talk and betting of the men.

"Wonder if old Dignam is going to enter Minkie this year?"

"Faix, an' if he does I bet the Little Warrhorrse will take the gimp out av her an' her runnin' mate."

"I'll bet three to one that my old Jen will pick the War-horse up before he passes the Grand Stand," growled a dog-man.

"An' it's meself will take thot bet in dollars," said Mickey, "an', moore than thot, Oi'll put up a hull month's stuff thot there ain't a dog in the mate thot kin turrn the Warrhorrse oncet on the hull coorse."

So they wrangled and wagered, but each day, as they put the Rabbits through their paces, there were more of those who believed that they had found a wonderful runner in the Warhorse, one that would give the best Greyhounds some-thing that is rarely seen, a straight stern chase from Start to Grand Stand and Haven.

6

The first morning of the meet arrived bright and promis-ing. The Grand Stand was filled with a city crowd. The usual types of a race-course appeared in force. Here and there were to be seen the dog-grooms leading in leash single Greyhounds or couples, shrouded in blankets, but showing their sinewy legs, their snaky necks, their shapely heads with long reptilian jaws, and their quick, nervous yellow eyes—hybrids of natural force and human ingenuity, the most wonderful runningmachines ever made of flesh and blood. Their keepers guarded them like jewels, tended them like babies, and were careful to keep them from picking up odd eatables, as well as prevent them smelling unusual objects or being approached by strangers. Large sums were wagered on these Dogs, and a cunningly placed tack, a piece of doctored meat, yes, an artfully compounded smell, has been known to turn a superb young runner into a lifeless laggard, and to the owner this might spell *ruin*. The Dogs entered in each class are paired off, as each contest is supposed to be a duel; the winners in the first series are then paired again. In each trial, a Jack is driven from the Starting-pen; close by in one leash are the rival Dogs, held by the slipper. As soon as the Hare is well away, the man has to get the Dogs evenly started and slip them together. On the field is the judge, scarlet-coated and well mounted. He follows the chase. The Hare, mindful of his training, speeds across the open, toward the Haven, in full view of the Grand Stand. The Dogs follow the Jack. As the first one comes near enough to be dangerous, the Hare balks him by dodging. Each time the Hare is turned, scores for the Dog that did it, and a final point is made by the kill.

Sometimes the kill takes place within one hundred yards of the start—that means a poor Jack; mostly it happens in front of the Grand Stand; but on rare occasions it chances that the Jack goes sailing across the open Park a good half-mile and, by dodging for time, runs to safety in the Haven. Four finishes are possible: a speedy kill; a speedy winning of the Haven; new Dogs to relieve the first runners, who would suffer heartcollapse in the terrific strain of their pace, if kept up many minutes in hot weather; and finally, for Rabbits that by continued dodging defy and jeopardize the Dogs, and yet do not win the Haven, there is kept a *loaded shotgun*.

There is just as much jockeying at a Kaskado coursing as at a Kaskado horse-race, just as many attempts at fraud, and it is just as necessary to have the judge and slipper beyond suspicion.

The day before the next meet a man of diamonds saw Irish Mickey—by chance. A cigar was all that visibly passed, but it had a green wrapper that was slipped off before lighting. Then a word: "If you wuz slipper to-morrow and it so came about that Dignam's Minkie gets done, wall,—it means another cigar."

"Faix, an' if I wuz slipper I could load the dice so Minkie would niver score a p'int, but her runnin' mate would have the same bad luck."

"That so?" The diamond man looked interested. "All right—fix it so; it means two cigars."

Slipper Slyman had always dealt on the square, had scorned many approaches—that was well known. Most believed in him, but there were some malcontents, and when a man with many gold seals approached the Steward and formulated charges, serious and well-backed, they must perforce suspend the slipper pending an inquiry, and thus Mickey Doo reigned in his stead.

Mickey was poor and not over-scrupulous. Here was a chance to make a year's pay in a minute, nothing wrong about it, no harm to the Dog or the Rabbit either.

One Jack-rabbit is much like another. Everybody knows that; it was simply a question of choosing your Jack.

The preliminaries were over. Fifty Jacks had been run and killed. Mickey had done his work satisfactorily; a fair slip had been given to every leash. He was still in command as slipper. Now came the final for the cup—the cup and the large stakes.

7

There were the slim and elegant Dogs awaiting their turn. Minkie and her rival were first. Everything had been fair so far, and who can say that what followed was unfair? Mickey could turn out which Jack he pleased.

"Number three!" he called to his partner.

Out leaped the Little Warhorse,—black and white his great ears, easy and low his five-foot bounds; gazing wildly at the unwonted crowd about the Park, he leaped high in one surprising spy-hop.

"Hrrrrr!" shouted the slipper, and his partner rattled a stick on the fence. The Warhorse's bounds increased to eight or nine feet.

"Hrrrrrr!" and they were ten or twelve feet. At thirty yards the Hounds were slipped—an even slip; some thought it could have been done at twenty yards.

"Hrrrrrr! Hrrrrrrr!" and the Warhorse was doing fourteen-foot leaps, not a spy-hop among them.

"Hrrrrr!" wonderful Dogs! how they sailed; but drifting ahead of them, like a white sea-bird or flying scud, was the Warhorse. Away past the Grand Stand. And the Dogs—were they closing the gap of start? Closing! It was lengthening! In less time than it takes to tell it, that black-and-white thistle-down had drifted away through the Haven door,—the door so like that good old hen-hole,—and the Greyhounds pulled up amidst a roar of derision and cheers for the Little Warhorse. How Mickey did laugh! How Dignam did swear! How the newspaper men did scribble—scribble—scribble!

Next day there was a paragraph in all the papers: "Wonderful Feat of a Jack-rabbit. The Little Warhorse, as he has been styled, completely skunked two of the most famous Dogs on the turf," etc.

There was a fierce wrangle among the dog-men. This was a tie, since neither had scored, and Minkie and her rival were allowed to run again; but that half-mile had been too hot, and they had no show for the cup.

Mickey met "Diamonds" next day, *by chance.*

"Have a cigar, Mickey."

"Oi will thot, sor. Faix, thim's so foine, I'd loike two—thank ye, sor."

8

From that time the Little Warhorse became the pride of the Irish boy. Slipper Slyman had been honorably reinstated and Mickey reduced to the rank of Jack-starter, but that merely helped to turn his sympathies from the Dogs to the Rabbits, or rather to the Warhorse, for of all the five hundred that were brought in from the drive he alone had won renown. There were several that crossed the Park to run again another day, but he alone had crossed the course without getting even a turn. Twice a week the meets took place; forty or fifty Jacks were killed each time, and the five hundred in the pen had been nearly all eaten out of the arena.

The Warhorse had run each day, and as often he had made the Haven. Mickey became wildly enthusiastic about his favorite's powers. He begot a positive affection for the clean-limbed racer, and stoutly maintained against all that it was a positive honor to a Dog to be disgraced by such a Jack.

It is so seldom that a Rabbit crosses the track at all, that when Jack did it six times without having to dodge, the papers took note of it, and after each meet there appeared a notice: "The Little Warhorse crossed again to-day; old-timers say it shows how our Dogs are deteriorating."

After the sixth time the rabbit-keepers grew enthusiastic, and Mickey, commander-in-chief of the brigade, became intemperate in his admiration. "Be jabers, he has a right to be torned loose. He has won his freedom loike ivery Amerikin done," he added, by way of appeal to the patriotism of the Steward of the race, who was, of course, the real owner of the Jacks.

"All right, Mick; if he gets across thirteen times you can ship him back to his native land," was the reply.

"Shure now, an' won't you make it tin, sor?"

"No, no; I need him to take the conceit out of some of the new Dogs that are coming."

"Thirteen toimes and he is free, sor; it's a bargain."

A new lot of Rabbits arrived about this time, and one of these was colored much like Little Warhorse. He had no such speed, but to prevent mistakes Mickey caught his favorite by driving him into one of the padded shipping-boxes, and proceeded with the gate-keeper's punch to earmark him. The punch was sharp; a clear star was cut out of the thin flap, when Mickey exclaimed: "Faix, an' Oi'll punch for ivery toime ye cross the coorse." So he cut six stars in a row. "Thayer now, Warrhorrse, shure it's a free Rabbit ye'll be when ye hove yer thirteen stars loike our flag of liberty hed when *we* got free."

Within a week the Warhorse had vanquished the new Greyhounds and had stars enough to go round the right ear and begin on the left. In a week more the thirteen runs were completed, six stars in the left ear and seven in the right, and the newspapers had new material.

"Whoop!" How Mickey hoorayed! "An' it's a free Jack ye are, Warrhorrse! Thirteen always wuz a lucky number. I never knowed it to fail."

9

"Yes, I know I did," said the Steward. "But I want to give him one more run. I have a bet on him against a new Dog here. It won't hurt him now; he can do it. Oh, well. Here now, Mickey, don't you get sassy. One run more this afternoon. The Dogs run two or three times a day; why not the Jack?"

"They're not shtakin' thayre loives, sor."

"Oh, you get out."

Many more Rabbits had been added to the pen,—big and small, peaceful and warlike,—and one big Buck of savage instincts, seeing Jack Warhorse's hurried dash into the Haven that morning, took advantage of the moment to attack him.

At another time Jack would have thumped his skull, as he once did the Cat's, and settled the affair in a minute; but now it took several minutes, during which he himself got roughly handled; so when the afternoon came he was suffering from one or two bruises and stiffening wounds; not serious, indeed, but enough to lower his speed.

The start was much like those of previous runs. The Warhorse steaming away low and lightly, his ears up and the breezes whistling through his thirteen stars.

Minkie with Fango, the new Dog, bounded in eager pursuit, but, to the surprise of the starters, the gap grew smaller. The Warhorse was losing ground, and right before the Grand Stand old Minkie turned him, and a cheer went up from the dog-men, for all knew the runners. Within fifty yards Fango scored a turn, and the race was right back to the start. There stood Slyman and Mickey. The Rabbit dodged, the Greyhounds plunged; Jack could not get away, and just as the final snap seemed near, the Warhorse leaped straight for

Mickey, and in an instant was hidden in his arms, while the starter's feet flew out in energetic kicks to repel the furious Dogs. It is not likely that the Jack knew Mickey for a friend; he only yielded to the old instinct to fly from a certain enemy to a neutral or a possible friend, and, as luck would have it, he had wisely leaped and well. A cheer went up from the benches as Mickey hurried back with his favorite. But the dog-men protested "it wasn't a fair run—they wanted it finished." They appealed to the Steward. He had backed the Jack against Fango. He was sore now, and ordered a new race.

An hour's rest was the best Mickey could get for him. Then he went as before, with Fango and Minkie in pursuit. He seemed less stiff now—he ran more like himself; but a little past the Stand he was turned by Fango and again by Minkie, and back and across, and here and there, leaping frantically and barely eluding his foes. For several minutes it lasted. Mickey could see that Jack's ears were sinking. The new Dog leaped. Jack dodged almost under him to escape, and back only to meet the second Dog; and now both ears were flat on his back. But the Hounds were suffering too. Their tongues were lolling out; their jaws and heaving sides were splashed with foam. The Warhorse's ears went up again. His courage seemed to revive in their distress. He made a straight dash for the Haven; but the straight dash was just what the Hounds could do, and within a hundred yards he was turned again, to begin another desperate game of zigzag. Then the dog-men saw danger for their Dogs, and two new ones were slipped—two fresh Hounds; surely they could end the race. *But they did not.* The first two were vanquished—gasping—out of it, but the next two were racing near. The Warhorse put forth all his strength. He left the first two far behind—

was nearly to the Haven when the second two came up.

Nothing but dodging could save him now. His ears were sinking, his heart was pattering on his ribs, but his spirit was strong. He flung himself in wildest zigzags. The Hounds tumbled over each other. Again and again they thought they had him. One of them snapped off the end of his long black tail, yet he escaped; but he could not get to the Haven. The luck was against him. He was forced nearer to the Grand Stand. A thousand ladies were watching. The time limit was up. The second Dogs were suffering, when Mickey came running, yelling like a madman—words—imprecations—crazy sounds:

"Ye blackguard hoodlums! Ye dhirty, cowardly bastes!" and he rushed furiously at the Dogs, intent to do them bodily harm.

Officers came running and shouting, and Mickey, shrieking hatred and defiance, was dragged from the field, reviling Dogs and men with every horrid, insulting name he could think of or invent.

"Fair play! Whayer's yer fair play, ye liars, ye dhirty cheats, ye bloody cowards!" And they drove him from the arena. The last he saw of it was the four foaming Dogs feebly dodging after a weak and worn-out Jack-rabbit, and the judge on his Horse beckoning to the man with the gun.

The gate closed behind him, and Mickey heard a *bang— bang,* an unusual uproar mixed with yelps of Dogs, and he knew that Little Jack Warhorse had been served with finish No. 4.

All his life he had loved Dogs, but his sense of fair play was outraged. He could not get in, nor see in from where he was. He raced along the lane to the Haven, where he might get a good view, and arrived in time to see—Little Jack Warhorse with his half-masted ears limp into the Haven;

and he realized at once that the man with the gun has missed, had hit the wrong runner, for there was the crowd at the Stand watching two men who were carrying a wounded Greyhound, while a veterinary surgeon was ministering to another that was panting on the ground.

Mickey looked about, seized a little shipping-box, put it at the angle of the Haven, carefully drove the tired thing into it, closed the lid, then, with the box under his arm, he scaled the fence unseen in the confusion and was gone.

'It didn't matter; he had lost his job anyway.' He tramped away from the city. He took the train at the nearest station and travelled some hours, and now he was in Rabbit country again. The sun had long gone down; the night with its stars was over the plain when among the farms, the Osage and alfalfa, Mickey Doo opened the box and gently put the Warhorse out.

Grinning as he did so, he said: "Shure an' it's ould Oireland thot's proud to set the thirteen stars at liberty wance moore."

For a moment the Little Warhorse gazed in doubt, then took three or four long leaps and a spy-hop to get his bearings. Now spreading his national colors and his honor-marked ears, he bounded into his hard-won freedom, strong as ever, and melted into the night of his native plain.

He has been seen many times in Kaskado, and there have been many Rabbit drives in that region, but he seems to know some means of baffling them now, for, in all the thousands that have been trapped and corralled, they have never since seen the star-spangled ears of Little Jack Warhorse.

Snap

THE STORY OF A BULL-TERRIER

Snap

1

I̶T was dusk on Hallowe'en when first I saw him. Early in the morning I had received a telegram from my college chum Jack: "Lest we forget. Am sending you a remarkable pup. Be polite to him; it's safer." It would have been just like Jack to have sent an infernal machine or a Skunk rampant and called it a pup, so I awaited the hamper with curiosity. When it arrived I saw it was marked "Dangerous," and there came from within a high-pitched snarl at every slight provocation. On peering through the wire netting I saw it was not a baby Tiger but a small white Bull-terrier. He snapped at me and at anyone or anything that seemed too abrupt or too near for proper respect, and his snarling growl was unpleasantly frequent. Dogs have two growls: one deep-rumbled, and chesty: that is polite warning—the retort courteous; the other mouthy and much higher in pitch: this is the last word before actual onslaught. The Terrier's growls were all of the latter kind. I was a dog-man and thought I knew all about Dogs, so, dismissing the porter I got out my all-round jackknife-toothpick-nailhammer-hatchet-toolbox-fire-shovel, a specialty of our firm, and lifted the netting. Oh, yes, I knew all about Dogs. The little fury had been growling out a whole-souled growl for every tap of the tool, and when I turned the box on its side, he made a dash straight for my legs. Had not his foot gone through the wire netting and held him, I might have been hurt, for his heart was evidently in his work; but I stepped on the table out of reach and tried to reason with him. I have always believed in talking to animals. I maintain that they gather something of our intention at least, even if they do not understand our words; but the Dog evidently put me down for a hypocrite and scorned my approaches.

At first he took his post under the table and kept up a circular watch for a leg trying to get down. I felt sure I could have controlled him with my eye, but I could not bring it to bear where I was, or rather where he was; thus I was left a prisoner. I am a very cool person, I flatter myself; in fact, I represent a hardware firm, and, in coolness, we are not excelled by any but perhaps the nosy gentlemen that sell wearing-apparel. I got out a cigar and smoked tailor-style on the table, while my little tyrant below kept watch for legs. I got out the telegram and read it: "Remarkable pup. Be polite to him; it's safer." I think it was my coolness rather than my politeness that did it, for in half an hour the growling ceased. In an hour he no longer jumped at a newspaper cautiously pushed over the edge to test his humor; possibly the irritation of the cage was wearing off, and by the time I had lit my third cigar, he waddled out to the fire and lay down; not ignoring me, however, I had no reason to complain of that kind of contempt. He kept one eye on me, and I kept both eyes, not on

him, but on his stump tail. If that tail should swing sidewise
once I should feel I was winning; but it did not swing. I got a
book and put in time on that table till my legs were cramped
and the fire burned low. About 10 P.M. it was chilly, and at
half-past ten the fire was out. My Hallowe'en present got up,
yawned and stretched, then walked under my bed, where he
found a fur rug. By stepping lightly from the table to the
dresser, and then on to the mantel-shelf, I also reached bed,
and, very quietly undressing, got in without provoking any
criticism from my master. I had not yet fallen asleep when
I heard a slight scrambling and felt "thump-thump" on the
bed, then over my feet and legs; Snap evidently had found
it too cool down below, and proposed to have the best my
house afforded.

He curled up on my feet in such a way that I was very
uncomfortable and tried to readjust matters, but the slightest
wriggle of my toe was enough to make him snap at it so
fiercely that nothing but thick woollen bedclothes saved me
from being maimed for life.

I was an hour moving my feet—a hair's-breadth at a time
—till they were so that I could sleep in comfort; and I was
awakened several times during the night by angry snarls from
the Dog—I suppose because I dared to move a toe without
his approval, though once I believe he did it simply because
I was snoring.

In the morning I was ready to get up before Snap was.
You see, I call him Snap—Gingersnap in full. Some Dogs
are hard to name, and some do not seem to need it—they
name themselves.

I was ready to rise at seven. Snap was not ready till eight,
so we rose at eight. He had little to say to the man who made

the fire. He allowed me to dress without doing it on the table. As I left the room to get breakfast, I remarked:

"Snap, my friend, some men would whip you into a different way, but I think I know a better plan. The doctors nowadays favor the 'no-breakfast cure.' I shall try that."

It seemed cruel, but I left him without food all day. It cost me something to repaint the door where he scratched it, but at night he was quite ready to accept a little food at my hands.

In a week we were very good friends. He would sleep on my bed now and allow me to move my feet without snapping at them, intent to do me serious bodily harm. The no-breakfast cure had worked wonders; in three months we were— well, simply man and Dog, and he amply justified the telegram he came with.

He seemed to be without fear. If a small Dog came near, he would not take the slightest notice; if a medium-sized Dog, he would stick his stub of a tail rigidly up in the air, then walk around him, scratching contemptuously with his hind feet, and looking at the sky, the distance, the ground, anything but the Dog, and noting his presence only by frequent high-pitched growls. If the stranger did not move on at once, the battle began, and then the stranger usually moved on very rapidly. Snap sometimes got worsted, but no amount of sad experience could ever inspire him with a grain of caution. Once, while riding in a cab during the Dog Show, Snap caught sight of an elephantine St. Bernard taking an airing. Its size aroused such enthusiasm in the Pup's little breast that he leaped from the cab window to do battle, and broke his leg.

Evidently fear had been left out of his make-up and its place supplied with an extra amount of ginger, which was the reason of his full name. He differed from all other Dogs I have ever known. For example, if a boy threw a stone at him, he ran, not away, but toward the boy, and if the crime was repeated, Snap took the law into his own hands; thus he was at least respected by all. Only myself and the porter at the office seemed to realize his good points, and we only were admitted to the high honor of personal friendship, an honor which I appreciated more as months went on, and by midsummer not Carnegie, Vanderbilt, and Astor together could have raised money enough to buy a quarter of a share in my little Dog Snap.

2

Though not a regular traveller, I was ordered out on the road in the autumn, and then Snap and the landlady were left together, with unfortunate developments. Contempt on his part—fear on hers; and hate on both.

I was placing a lot of barb-wire in the northern tier of States. My letters were forwarded once a week, and I got several complaints from the landlady about Snap.

Arrived at Mendoza, in North Dakota, I found a fine market for wire. Of course my dealings were with the big storekeepers, but I went about among the ranchmen to get their practical views on the different styles, and thus I met the Penroof Brothers' Cow-outfit.

One cannot be long in Cow country now without hearing a great deal about the depredations of the ever wily and destructive Gray-wolf. The day has gone by when they can be poisoned wholesale, and they are a serious drain on the

rancher's profits. The Penroof Brothers, like most live cattle-
men, had given up all attempts at poisoning and trapping,
and were trying various breeds of Dogs as Wolf-hunters, hoping to get a little sport out of the necessary work of destroying the pests.

Foxhounds had failed—they were too soft for fighting;
Great Danes were too clumsy, and Greyhounds could not
follow the game unless they could see it. Each breed had
some fatal defect, but the cow-men hoped to succeed with a
mixed pack, and the day when I was invited to join in a
Mendoza Wolf-hunt, I was amused by the variety of Dogs
that followed. There were several mongrels, but there were
also a few highly bred Dogs—in particular, some Russian
Wolfhounds that must have cost a lost of money.

Hilton Penroof, the oldest boy, "The Master of Hounds,"
was unusually proud of them, and expected them to do great
things.

"Greyhounds are too thin-skinned to fight a Wolf, Danes
are too slow, but you'll see the fur fly when the Russians take
a hand."

Thus the Greyhounds were there as runners, the Danes
as heavy backers, and the Russians to do the important fighting. There were also two or three Foxhounds, whose fine
noses were relied on to follow the trail if the game got out
of view.

It was a fine sight as we rode away among the Badland
Buttes that October day. The air was bright and crisp, and
though so late, there was neither snow nor frost. The Horses
were fresh, and once or twice showed me how a Cow-pony
tries to get rid of his rider.

The Dogs were keen for sport, and we did start one or

two gray spots in the plain that Hilton said were Wolves or Coyotes. The Dogs trailed away at full cry, but at night, beyond the fact that one of the Greyhounds had a wound on his shoulder, there was nothing to show that any of them had been on a Wolf-hunt.

"It's my opinion yer fancy Russians is no good, Hilt," said Garvin, the younger brother. "I'll back that little black Dane against the lot, mongrel an' all as he is."

"I don't unnerstan' it," growled Hilton. "There ain't a Coyote, let alone a Gray-wolf, kin run away from them Greyhounds; them Foxhounds kin folly a trail three days old, an' the Danes could lick a Grizzly."

"I reckon," said the father, "they kin run, an' they kin track, an' they kin lick a Grizzly, *maybe,* but the fac' is they don't want to tackle a Gray-wolf. The hull darn pack is scairt—an' I wish we had our money out o' them."

Thus the men grumbled and discussed as I drove away and left them.

There seemed only one solution of the failure. The Hounds were swift and strong, but a Gray-wolf seems to terrorize all Dogs. They have not the nerve to face him, and so, each time he gets away, and my thoughts flew back to the fearless little Dog that had shared my bed for the last year. How I wished he was out here, then these lubberly giants of Hounds would find a leader whose nerve would not fail at the moment of trial.

At Baroka, my next stop, I got a batch of mail including two letters from the landlady; the first to say that "that beast of a Dog was acting up scandalous in my room," and the other still more forcible, demanding his immediate removal.

"Why not have him expressed to Mendoza?" I thought.

"It's only twenty hours; they'll be glad to have him. I can take him home with me when I go through."

3

My next meeting with Gingersnap was not as different from the first as one might have expected. He jumped on me, made much vigorous pretense to bite, and growled frequently, but it was a deep-chested growl and his stump waggled hard.

The Penroofs had had a number of Wolf-hunts since I was with them, and were much disgusted at having no better success than before. The Dogs could find a Wolf nearly every time they went out, but they could not kill him, and the men were not near enough at the finish to learn why.

Old Penroof was satisfied that "thar wasn't one of the hull miserable gang that had the grit of a Jack-rabbit."

We were off at dawn the next day—the same procession of fine Horses and superb riders; the big blue Dogs, the yellow Dogs, the spotted Dogs, as before; but there was a new feature, a little white Dog that stayed close by me, and not only any Dogs, but Horses that came too near were apt to get a surprise from his teeth. I think he quarrelled with every man, Horse, and Dog in the country, with the exception of a Bull-terrier belonging to the Mendoza hotel man. She was the only one smaller than himself, and they seemed very good friends.

I shall never forget the view of the hunt I had that day. We were on one of those large, flat-headed buttes that give a kingdom to the eye, when Hilton, who had been scanning the vast country with glasses, exclaimed: "I see him. There he goes, toward Skull Creek. Guess it's a Coyote."

Now the first thing is to get the Greyhounds to see the prey —not an easy matter, as they cannot use the glasses, and the ground was covered with sage-brush higher than the Dogs' heads.

But Hilton called, "Hu, hu, Dander," and leaned aside from his saddle, holding out his foot at the same time. With one agile bound Dander leaped to the saddle and there stood balancing on the Horse while Hilton kept pointing. "There he is, Dander; sic him—see him down there." The Dog gazed earnestly where his master pointed, then seeming to see, he sprang to the ground with a slight yelp and sped way. The other Dogs followed after, in an ever-lengthening procession, and we rode as hard as we could behind them, but losing time, for the ground was cut with gullies, spotted with badger-holes, and covered with rocks and sage that made full speed too hazardous.

We all fell behind, and I was last, of course, being least accustomed to the saddle. We got several glimpses of the Dogs flying over the level plain or dropping from sight in gullies to reappear at the other side. Dander, the Greyhound, was the recognized leader, and as we mounted another ridge we got sight of the whole chase—a Coyote at full speed, the Dogs a quarter of a mile behind, but gaining. When next we saw them the Coyote was dead, and the Dogs sitting around panting, all but two of the Foxhounds and Gingersnap.

"Too late for the fracas," remarked Hilton, glancing at these last Foxhounds. Then he proudly petted Dander. "Didn't need yer purp after all, ye see."

"Takes a heap of nerve for ten big Dogs to face one little

Coyote," remarked the father, sarcastically. "Wait till we run onto a Gray."

Next day we were out again, for I made up my mind to see it to a finish.

From a high point we caught sight of a moving speck of gray. A moving white speck stands for Antelope, a red speck for Fox, a gray speck for either Gray-wolf or Coyote, and which of these is determined by its tail. If the glass shows the tail down, it is a Coyote; if up, it is the hated Gray-wolf.

Dander was shown the game as before and led the motley mixed procession—as he had before—Greyhounds, Wolf-hounds, Foxhounds, Danes, Bull-terrier, horsemen. We got a momentary view of the pursuit; a Gray-wolf it surely was, lop-ing away ahead of the Dogs. Somehow I thought the first Dogs were not running so fast now as they had after the Coyote. But no one knew the finish of the hunt. The Dogs came back to us one by one, and we saw no more of that Wolf.

Sarcastic remarks and recrimination were now freely in-dulged in by the hunters.

"Pah! scairt, plumb scairt," was the father's disgusted com-ment on the pack. "They could catch up easy enough, but when he turned on them, they lighted out for home—pah!"

"Where's that thar onsurpassable, fearless, scaired-o'-nort Tarrier?" asked Hilton, scornfully.

"I don't know," said I. "I am inclined to think he never saw the Wolf; but if he ever does, I'll bet he sails in for death or glory."

That night several Cows were killed close to the ranch, and we were spurred on to another hunt.

It opened much like the last. Late in the afternoon we sighted a gray fellow with tail up, not half a mile off. Hilton called Dander up on the saddle. I acted on the idea and called Snap to mine. His legs were so short that he had to leap several times before he made it, scrambling up at last with my foot as a half-way station. I pointed and "sic-ed" for a minute before he saw the game, and then he started out after the Greyhounds, already gone, with energy that was full of promise.

The chase this time led us, not to the rough brakes along the river, but toward the high open country, for reasons that appeared later. We were close together as we rose to the upland and sighted the chase half a mile off, just as Dander came up with the Wolf and snapped at his haunch. The Gray-wolf turned round to fight, and we had a fine view. The Dogs came up by twos and threes, barking at him in a ring, till last the little white one rushed up. He wasted no time barking, but rushed straight at the Wolf's throat and missed it, yet seemed to get him by the nose; then the ten big Dogs closed in, and in two minutes the Wolf was dead. We had ridden hard to be in at the finish, and though our view was distant, we saw at least that Snap had lived up to the telegram, as well as to my promises for him.

Now it was my turn to crow, and I did not lose the chance. Snap had shown them how, and at last the Mendoza pack had killed a Gray-wolf without help from the men.

There were two things to mar the victory somewhat; first, it was a young Wolf, a mere Cub, hence his foolish choice of country; second, Snap was wounded—the Wolf had given him a bad cut in the shoulder.

As we rode in proud procession home, I saw he limped a little. "Here," I cried, "come up, Snap." He tried once or twice to jump to the saddle, but could not. "Here, Hilton, lift him up to me."

"Thanks; I'll let you handle your own rattlesnakes," was the reply, for all knew now that it was not safe to meddle with his person. "Here, Snap, take hold," I said, and held my quirt to him. He seized it, and by that I lifted him on the front of my saddle and so carried him home. I cared for him as though he had been a baby. He had shown those Cattle-men how to fill the weak place in their pack; the Foxhounds may be good and the Greyhounds swift and the Russians and Danes fighters, but they are no use at all without the crowning moral force of grit, that none can supply so well as a Bull-terrier. On that day the Cattle-men learned how to manage the Wolf question, as you will find if ever you are at Mendoza; for every successful Wolf pack there has with it a Bull-terrier, preferably of the Snap-Mendoza breed.

4

Next day was Hallowe'en, the anniversary of Snap's advent, The weather was clear, bright, not too cold, and there was no snow on the ground. The men usually celebrated the day with a hunt of some sort, and now, of course, Wolves were the one object. To the disappointment of all, Snap was in bad shape with his wound. He slept, as usual, at my feet, and bloody stains now marked the place. He was not in condition to fight, but we were bound to have a Wolf-hunt, so he was beguiled to an outhouse and locked up, while we went off, I, at least, with a sense of impending disaster. I *knew* we should fail without my Dog, but I did not realize how bad a failure it was to be.

Afar among the buttes of Skull Creek we had roamed when

a white ball appeared bounding through the sage-brush, and in a minute more Snap came, growling and stump-waggling, up to my Horse's side. I could not send him back; he would take no such orders, not even from me. His wound was looking bad, so I called him, held down the quirt, and jumped him to my saddle.

"There," I thought, "I'll keep you safe till we get home." Yes, I thought; but I reckoned not with Snap. The voice of Hilton, "Hu, hu," announced that he had sighted a Wolf. Dander and Riley, his rival, both sprang to the point of observation, with the result that they collided and fell together, sprawling, in the sage. But Snap, gazing hard, had sighted the Wolf, not so very far off, and before I knew it, he leaped from the saddle and bounded zigzag, high, low, in and under the sage, straight for the enemy, leading the whole pack for a few minutes. Not far, of course. The great Greyhounds sighted the moving speck, and the usual procession strung out on the plain. It promised to be a fine hunt, for the Wolf had less than half a mile start and all the Dogs were fully interested.

"They've turned up Grizzly Gully," cried Garvin. "This way, and we can head them off."

So we turned and rode hard around the north side of Hulmer's Butte, while the chase seemed to go round the south.

We galloped to the top of Cedar Ridge and were about to ride down, when Hilton shouted, "By George, here he is! We're right onto him." He leaped from his Horse, dropped the bridle, and ran forward. I did the same. A great Gray-wolf came lumbering across an open plain toward us. His head was low, his tail out level, and fifty yards behind him was Dander, sailing like a Hawk over the ground, going twice as fast as the Wolf. In a minute the Hound was alongside and snapped, but bounded back, as the Wolf turned on him. They were just below us now and not fifty feet away. Garvin drew his revolver, but in a fateful moment Hilton interfered: "No; no; let's see it out." In a few seconds the next Greyhound arrived, then the rest in order of swiftness. Each came up full of fight and fury, determined to go right in and tear the Gray-wolf to pieces; but each in turn swerved aside, and leaped and barked around at a safe distance. After a minute or so the Russians appeared—fine big Dogs they were. Their distant intention no doubt was to dash right at the old Wolf; but his fearless front, his sinewy frame and death-dealing jaws, awed them long before they were near him, and they also joined the ring, while the desperado in the middle faced this way and that, ready for any or all.

Now the Danes came up, huge-limbed creatures, any one of them as heavy as the Wolf. I heard their heavy breathing tighten into a threatening sound as they plunged ahead, eager to tear the foe to pieces; but when they saw him there, grim fearless, mighty of jaw, tireless of limb, ready to die if need be, but sure of this, he would not die alone—well, those great Danes—all three of them—were stricken, as the rest had been, with a sudden bashfulness: yes, they would go right in presently—not now, but as soon as they had got their breath; they were not afraid of a Wolf, oh no. I could read their courage in their voices. They knew perfectly well that the first Dog to go in was going to get hurt, but never mind that—presently; they would bark a little more to get up enthusiasm.

And as the ten big Dogs were leaping round the silent Wolf at bay, there was a rustling in the sage at the far side of the place; then a snow-white rubber ball, it seemed, came bounding, but grew into a little Bull-terrier, and Snap, slowest of the pack, and last, came panting hard, so hard he seemed gasping. Over the level open he made, straight to the changing ring around the Cattle-killer who none dared face. Did he hesitate. Not for an instant; through the ring of the yelping pack, straight for the old despot of the range, right for his throat, he sprang; and the Gray-wolf struck with his twenty scimitars. But the little one, if foiled at all, sprang again, and then what came I hardly knew. There was a whirling mass of Dogs. I thought I saw the little White One clinched on the Gray-wolf's nose. The pack was all around; we could not help them now. But they did not need us; they had a leader of dauntless mettle, and when in a little while the final scene was done, there on the ground lay the Gray-wolf, a giant of his kind, and clinched on his nose was the little white Dog.

We were standing around within fifteen feet, ready to help, but had no chance till we were not needed.

The Wolf was dead, and I hallooed to Snap, but he did not move. I bent over him. "Snap—Snap, it's all over; you've killed him." But the Dog was very still, and now I saw two deep wounds in his body. I tried to lift him. "Let go, old fellow; it's all over." He growled feebly, and at last let go of the Wolf. The rough Cattle-men were kneeling around him now; old Penroof's voice was trembling as he muttered, "I wouldn't had him hurt for twenty steers." I lifted him in my arms, called to him and stroked his head. He snarled a little, a farewell as it proved, for he licked my hand as he did so, then never snarled again.

That was a sad ride home for me. There was the skin of a monstrous Wolf, but no other hint of triumph. We buried the fearless one on a butte back of the ranch-house. Penroof, as he stood by, was heard to grumble: "By jingo, that was grit—cl'ar grit! Ye can't raise Cattle without grit."

The Winnipeg Wolf

The Winnipeg Wolf

T was during the great blizzard of 1882 that I first met the Winnipeg Wolf. I had left St. Paul in the middle of March to cross the prairies to Winnipeg, expecting to be there in twenty-four hours, but the Storm King had planned it otherwise and sent a heavy-laden eastern blast. The snow came down in a furious, steady torrent, hour after hour. Never before had I seen such a storm. All the world was lost in snow —snow, snow, snow—whirling, biting, stinging, drifting snow —and the puffing, monstrous engine was compelled to stop at the command of those tiny, feathery crystals of spotless purity.

Many strong hands with shovels came to the delicately curled snowdrifts that barred our way, and in an hour the engine could pass—only to stick in another drift yet farther on. It was dreary work—day after day, night after night, sticking in the drifts, digging ourselves out, and still the snow went whirling and playing about us.

"Twenty-two hours to Emerson," said the official, but nearly two weeks of digging passed before we did reach Emer-

son, and the poplar country where the thickets stop all drifting of the snow. Thenceforth the train went swiftly, the poplar woods grew more thickly—we passed for miles through
solid forests, then perhaps through an open space. As we
neared St. Boniface, the eastern outskirts of Winnipeg, we
dashed across a little glade fifty yards wide, and there in the
middle was a group that stirred me to the very soul.

In plain view was a great rabble of Dogs, large and small,
black, white, and yellow, wriggling and heaving this way and
that way in a rude ring; to one side was a little yellow Dog
stretched and quiet in the snow; on the outer part of the ring
was a huge black Dog bounding about and barking, but keeping ever behind the moving mob. And in the midst, the center
and cause of it all, was a great, grim Wolf.

Wolf? He looked like a Lion. There he stood, all alone—
resolute—calm—with bristling mane, and legs braced firmly,
glancing this way and that, to be ready for an attack in any
direction. There was a curl on his lips—it looked like scorn,
but I suppose it was really the fighting snarl of tooth display.
Led by a wolfish-looking Dog that should have been ashamed,
the pack dashed in, for the twentieth time no doubt. But the
great gray form leaped here and there, and chop, chop, chop
went those fearful jaws, no other sound from the lonely warrior; but a death yelp from more than one of his foes, as those
that were able again sprang back, and left him statuesque as
before, untamed, unmaimed, and contemptuous of them all.

How I wished for the train to stick in a snowdrift now, as so
often before, for all my heart went out to that Gray-wolf; I
longed to go and help him. But the snow-deep glade flashed
by, the poplar trunks shut out the view, and we went on to
our journey's end.

This was all I saw, and it seemed little; but before many days had passed I knew surely that I had been favored with a view, in broad daylight, of a rare and wonderful creature, none less than the Winnipeg Wolf.

His was a strange history—a Wolf that preferred the city to the country, that passed by the Sheep to kill the Dogs, and that always hunted alone.

In telling the story of *le Garou,* as he was called by some, although I speak of these things as locally familiar, it is very sure that to many citizens of the town they were quite unknown. The smug shopkeeper on the main street had scarcely heard of him until the day after the final scene at the slaughterhouse, when his great carcass was carried to Hine's taxidermist shop and there mounted, to be exhibited later at the Chicago World's Fair, and to be destroyed, alas! in the fire that reduced the Mulvey Grammar School to ashes in 1896.

2

It seems that Fiddler Paul, the handsome ne'er-do-well of the half-breed world, readier to hunt than to work, was prowling with his gun along the wooded banks of the Red River by Kildonan, one day in the June of 1880. He saw a Gray-wolf come out of a hole in a bank and fired a chance shot that killed it. Having made sure, by sending in his Dog, that no other large Wolf was there, he crawled into the den, and found, to his utter amazement and delight, eight young Wolves—nine bounties of ten dollars each. How much is that? A fortune surely. He used a stick vigorously, and with the assistance of the yellow Cur, all the little ones were killed but one. There is a superstition about the last of a brood—it is not lucky to kill it. So Paul set out for town with the scalp of the old Wolf, the scalps of the seven young, and the last Cub alive.

The saloon-keeper, who got the dollars for which the scalps were exchanged, soon got the living Cub. He grew up at the end of a chain, but developed a chest and jaws that no Hound in town could match. He was kept in the yard for the amusement of customers, and this amusement usually took the form of baiting the captive with Dogs. The young Wolf was bitten and mauled nearly to death on several occasions, but he recovered, and each month there were fewer Dogs willing to face him. His life was as hard as it could be. There was but one gleam of gentleness in it all, and that was the friendship that grew up between himself and Little Jim, the son of the saloon-keeper.

Jim was a wilful little rascal with a mind of his own. He took to the Wolf because it had killed a Dog that had bitten him. He thenceforth fed the Wolf and made a pet of it, and the Wolf responded by allowing him to take liberties which no one else dared venture.

Jim's father was not a model parent. He usually spoiled his son, but at times would get in a rage and beat him cruelly for some trifle. The child was quick to learn that he was beaten, not because he had done wrong, but because he had made his father angry. If, therefore, he could keep out of the way until that anger had cooled, he had no further cause for worry. One day, seeking safety in flight with his father behind him, he dashed into the Wolf's kennel, and his grizzly chum thus unceremoniously awakened turned to the door, displayed a double row of ivories, and plainly said to the father: "Don't you dare to touch him."

If Hogan could have shot the Wolf then and there he would have done so, but the chances were about equal of killing his son, so he let them alone and, half an hour later, laughed at the whole affair. Thenceforth Little Jim made for the Wolf's den whenever he was in danger, and sometimes the only notice any one had that the boy had been in mischief was seeing him sneak in behind the savage captive.

Economy in hired help was a first principle with Hogan. Therefore his "barkeep" was a Chinaman. He was a timid, harmless creature, so Paul des Roches did not hesitate to bully him. One day, finding Hogan out, and the Chinaman alone in charge, Paul, already tipsy, demanded a drink on credit, and Tung Ling, acting on standing orders, refused. His artless explanation, "No good, neber pay," so far from clearing up the difficulty, brought Paul staggering back of the bar to avenge the insult. The Celestial might have suffered grievous bodily hurt, but that Little Jim was at hand and had a long stick, with which he adroitly tripped up the Fiddler and sent him sprawling. He staggered to his feet swearing he would have Jim's life. But the child was near the back door and soon found refuge in the Wolf's kennel.

Seeing that the boy had a protector, Paul got the long stick, and from a safe distance began to belabor the Wolf. The grizzly creature raged at the end of the chain, but, though he parried many cruel blows by seizing the stick in his teeth, he was suffering severely, when Paul realized that Jim, whose tongue had not been idle, was fumbling away with nervous fingers to set the Wolf loose, and soon would succeed. Indeed, it would have been done already but for the strain that the Wolf kept on the chain.

The thought of being in the yard at the mercy of the huge

animal that he had so enraged, gave the brave Paul a thrill of terror.

Jim's wheedling voice was heard—"Hold on now, Wolfie; back up just a little, and you shall have him. Now do; there's a good Wolfie"—that was enough; the Fiddler fled and carefully closed all doors behind him.

Thus the friendship between Jim and his pet grew stronger, and the Wolf, as he developed his splendid natural powers, gave daily evidence also of the mortal hatred he bore to men that smelt of whiskey and to all Dogs, the causes of his sufferings. This peculiarity, coupled with his love for the child—and all children seemed to be included to some extent—grew with his growth and seemed to prove the ruling force of his life.

3

At this time—that is, the fall of 1881—there were great complaints among the Qu'Appelle ranchmen that the Wolves were increasing in their country and committing great depredations among the stock. Poisoning and trapping had proved failures, and when a distinguished German visitor appeared at the Club in Winnipeg and announced that he was bringing some Dogs that could easily rid the country of Wolves, he was listened to with unusual interest. For the Cattle-men are fond of sport, and the idea of helping their business by establishing a kennel of Wolfhounds was very alluring.

The German soon produced as samples of his Dogs, two magnificent Danes, one white, the other blue with black spots and a singular white eye that completed an expression of

unusual ferocity. Each of these great creatures weighed nearly
two hundred pounds. They were muscled like Tigers, and the
German was readily believed when he claimed that these two
alone were more than a match for the biggest Wolf. He thus
described their method of hunting: "All you have to do is
show them the trail and, even if it is a day old, away they go
on it. They cannot be shaken off. They will soon find that
Wolf, no matter how he doubles and hides. Then they close
on him. He turns to run, the blue Dog takes him by the
haunch and throws him like this," and the German jerked a
roll of bread into the air; "then before he touches the ground
the white Dog has his head, the other his tail, and they pull
him apart like that."

It sounded all right; at any rate every one was eager to put
it to the proof. Several of the residents said there was a fair
chance of finding a Gray-wolf along the Assiniboine, so a hunt
was organized. But they searched in vain for three days and
were giving it up when some one suggested that down at Hogan's saloon was a Wolf chained up, that they could get for the
value of the bounty, and though little more than a year old he
would serve to show what the Dogs could do.

The value of Hogan's Wolf went up at once when he knew
the importance of the occasion; besides, "he had conscientious
scruples." All his scruples vanished, however, when his views
as to price were met. His first care was to get Little Jim out of
the way by sending him on an errand to his grandma's; then
the Wolf was driven into his box and nailed in. The box was
put in a wagon and taken to the open prairie along the Por-
tage trail.

The Dogs could scarcely be held back, they were so eager
for the fray, as soon as they smelt the Wolf. But several strong

men held their leash, the wagon was drawn half a mile farther, and the Wolf was turned out with some difficulty. At first he looked scared and sullen. He tried to get out of sight, but made no attempt to bite. However, on finding himself free, as well as hissed and hooted at, he started off at a slinking trot toward the south, where the land seemed broken. The Dogs were released at that moment, and, baying furiously, they bounded away after the young Wolf. The men cheered loudly and rode behind them. From the very first it was clear that he had no chance. The Dogs were much swifter; the white one could run like a Greyhound. The German was wildly enthusiastic as she flew across the prairie, gaining visibly on the Wolf at every second. Many bets were offered on the Dogs, but there were no takers. The only bets accepted were Dog against Dog. The young Wolf went at speed now, but within a mile the white Dog was right behind him—was closing in.

The German shouted: "Now watch and see that Wolf go up in the air."

In a moment the runners were together. Both recoiled, neither went up in the air, but the white Dog rolled over with a fearful gash in her shoulder—out of the fight, if not killed. Ten seconds later the Blue-spot arrived, open-mouthed. This meeting was as quick and almost as mysterious as the first. The animals barely touched each other. The gray one bounded aside, his head out of sight for a moment in the flash of quick movement. Spot reeled and showed a bleeding flank. Urged on by the men, he assaulted again, but only to get another wound that taught him to keep off.

Now came the keeper with four more huge Dogs. They turned these loose, and the men armed with clubs and lassos were closing to help in finishing the Wolf, when a small boy came charging over the plain on a Pony. He leaped to the ground and wriggling through the ring flung his arms around the Wolf's neck. He called him his "Wolfie pet," his "dear Wolfie"—the Wolf licked his face and wagged its tail—then the child turned on the crowd and through his streaming tears, he— Well! it would not do to print what he said. He was only nine, but he was very old-fashioned, as well as a rude little boy. He had been brought up in a low saloon, and had been an apt pupil at picking up the vile talk of the place. He cursed them one and all and for generations back; he did not spare even his own father.

If a man had used such shocking and insulting language he might have been lynched, but coming from a baby, the hunters did not know what to do, so finally did the best thing. They laughed aloud—not at themselves, that is not considered good form—but they all laughed at the German whose wonderful Dogs had been worsted by a half-grown Wolf.

Jimmie now thrust his dirty, tear-stained little fist down into his very-much-of-a-boy's pocket, and from among marbles and chewing-gum, as well as tobacco, matches, pistol cartridges, and other contraband, he fished out a flimsy bit of grocer's twine and fastened it around the Wolf's neck. Then, still blubbering a little, he set out for home on the Pony, leading the Wolf and hurling a final threat and anathema at the German nobleman: "Fur two cents I'd sic him on *you,* gol darn ye."

4

Early that winter Jimmie was taken down with a fever. The

Wolf howled miserably in the yard when he missed his little friend, and finally on the boy's demand was admitted to the sick-room, and there this great wild Dog—for that is all a Wolf is—continued faithfully watching by his friend's bedside.

The fever had seemed slight at first, so that every one was shocked when there came suddenly a turn for the worse, and three days before Christmas Jimmie died. He had no more sincere mourner than his "Wolfie." The great gray creature howled in miserable answer to the church-bell tolling when he followed the body on Christmas Eve to the graveyard at St. Boniface. He soon came back to the premises behind the saloon, but when an attempt was made to chain him again, he leaped a board fence and was finally lost sight of.

Later that same winter old Renaud, the trapper, with his pretty half-breed daughter, Ninette, came to live in a little log-cabin on the river bank. He knew nothing about Jimmie Hogan, and he was not a little puzzled to find Wolf tracks and signs along the river on both sides between St. Boniface and Fort Garry. He listened with interest and doubt to tales that the Hudson Bay Company's men told of a great Gray-wolf that had come to live in the region about, and even to enter the town at night, and that was in particular attached to the woods about St. Boniface Church.

On Christmas Eve of that year when the bell tolled again as it had done for Jimmie, a lone and melancholy howling from the woods almost convinced Renaud that the stories were true. He knew the wolf-cries—the howl for help, the love song, the lonely wail, and the sharp defiance of the Wolves. This was the lonely wail.

The trapper went to the riverside and gave an answering howl. A shadowy form left the far woods and crossed on the ice to where the man sat, log-still, on a log. It came up near him, circled past and sniffed, then its eye glowed; it growled like a Dog that is a little angry, and glided back into the night.

Thus Renaud knew, and before long many townfolk began to learn, that a huge Gray-wolf was living in their streets, "a Wolf three times as big as the one that used to be chained at Hogan's gin-mill." He was the terror of Dogs, killing them on all possible occasions, and some said, though it was never proven, that he had devoured more than one half-breed who was out on a spree.

And this was the Winnipeg Wolf that I had seen that day in the wintry woods. I had longed to go to his help, thinking the odds so hopelessly against him, but later knowledge changed the thought. I do not know how that fight ended, but I do know that he was seen many times afterward and some of the Dogs were not.

Thus his was the strangest life that ever his kind had known. Free of all the woods and plains, he elected rather to lead a life of daily hazard in the town—each week at least some close escape, and every day a day of daring deeds; finding momentary shelter at times under the very boardwalk crossings. Hating the men and despising the Dogs, he fought his daily way and held the hordes of Curs at bay or slew them when he found them few or single; harried the drunkard, evaded men with guns, learned traps—learned poison, too— just how, we cannot tell, but learn it he did, for he passed it again and again, or served it only with a Wolf's contempt.

Not a street in Winnipeg that he did not know; not a policeman in Winnipeg that had not seen his swift and shadowy form in the gray dawn as he passed where he would; not a Dog in Winnipeg that did not cower and bristle when the tell-tale wind brought proof that old Garou was crouching near. His only path was the warpath, and all the world his foes. But throughout this lurid, semi-mythic record there was one recurring pleasant thought—Garou never was known to harm a child.

5

Ninette was a desert-born beauty like her Indian mother, but gray-eyed like her Normandy father, a sweet girl of sixteen, the belle of her set. She might have married any one of the richest and steadiest young men of the country, but of course, in feminine perversity her heart was set on that ne'er-do-well, Paul des Roches. A handsome fellow, a good dancer and a fair violinist, Fiddler Paul was in demand at all festivities, but he was a shiftless drunkard and it was even whispered that he had a wife already in Lower Canada. Renaud very properly dismissed him when he came to urge his suit, but dismissed him in vain. Ninette, obedient in all else, would not give up her lover. The very day after her father had ordered him away she promised to meet him in the woods just across the river. It was easy to arrange this, for she was a good Catholic, and across the ice to the church was shorter than going around by the bridge. As she went through the snowy wood to the tryst she noticed that a large gray Dog was following. It seemed quite friendly, and the child (for she was still that) had no fear, but when she came to the place where Paul was waiting, the gray Dog went forward rumbling in its chest. Paul gave one look, knew it for a huge Wolf, then fled like the coward he was. He afterward said he ran for his gun. He must have forgotten where it was, as he climbed the nearest tree to find it. Meanwhile Ninette ran home across the ice to tell Paul's friends of his danger. Not finding any firearms up the tree, the valiant lover made a spear by fastening his knife to a branch and succeeded in giving Garou a painful wound on the head. The savage creature growled horribly but thenceforth kept at a safe distance, though plainly showing his intention to wait till the man came down. But the approach of a band of rescuers changed his mind, and he went away.

Fiddler Paul found it easier to explain matters to Ninette than he would to any one else. He still stood first in her affections, but so hopelessly ill with her father that they decided on an elopement, as soon as he should return from Fort Alexander, whither he was to go for the Company, as dog-driver. The Factor was very proud of his trained Dogs—three great Huskies with curly, bushy tails, big and strong as Calves, but fierce and lawless as pirates. With these the Fiddler Paul was to drive to Fort Alexander from Fort Garry—the bearer of several important packets. He was an expert Dog-driver, which usually means relentlessly cruel. He set off blithely down the river in the morning, after the several necessary drinks of whiskey. He expected to be gone a week, and would then come back with twenty dollars in his pocket, and having thus provided the sinews of war, would carry out the plan of elopement. Away they went down the river on the ice. The big Dogs pulled swiftly but sulkily as he cracked the long whip and shouted, *"Allez, allez, marchez."* They passed at speed by Renaud's shanty on the bank, and Paul, cracking his whip and running behind the train, waved his hand to Ninette as she stood by the door. Speedily the cariole with the sulky Dogs and drunken driver disappeared around the bend —and that was the last ever seen of Fiddler Paul.

That evening the Huskies came back singly to Fort Garry.

They were spattered with frozen blood, and were gashed in several places. But strange to tell they were quite "unhungry."

Runners went on the back trail and recovered the packages. They were lying on the ice unharmed. Fragments of the sled were strewn for a mile or more up the river; not far from the packages were shreds of clothing that had belonged to the Fiddler.

It was quite clear, the Dogs had murdered and eaten their driver.

The Factor was terribly wrought up over the matter. It might cost him his Dogs. He refused to believe the report and set off to sift the evidence for himself. Renaud was chosen to go with him, and before they were within three miles of the fatal place Renaud pointed to a very large track crossing from the east to the west bank of the river, just after the Dog sled. He ran it backward for a mile or more on the eastern bank, noted how it had walked when the Dogs walked and run when they ran, before he turned to the Factor and said: "A beeg Voolf—he come after ze cariole all ze time."

Now they followed the track where it had crossed to the west shore. Two miles above Kildonan woods the Wolf had stopped his gallop to walk over to the sled trail, had followed it a few yards, then had returned to the woods.

"Paul he drop somesin' here, ze packet maybe, ze Voolf he come for smell. He follow so—now he know zat eez ze drunken Paul vot slash heem on ze head."

A mile farther the Wolf track came galloping on the ice behind the cariole. The man track disappeared now, for the driver had leaped on the sled and lashed the Dogs. Here is where he cut adrift the bundles. That is why things were scattered over the ice. See how the Dogs were bounding under the lash. Here was the Fiddler's knife in the snow. He must have dropped it in trying to use it on the Wolf. And here—what! the Wolf track disappears, but the sled track speeds along. The Wolf has leaped on the sled. The Dogs, in terror, added to their speed; but on the sleigh behind them there is a deed of vengeance done. In a moment it is over; both roll off the sled; the Wolf track reappears on the east side to seek the woods. The sled swerves to the west bank, where, after half a mile, it is caught and wrecked on a root.

The snow also told Renaud how the Dogs, entangled in the harness, had fought with each other, had cut themselves loose, and trotting homeward by various ways up the river, had gathered at the body of their late tyrant and devoured him at a meal.

Bad enough for the Dogs, still they were cleared of the murder. That certainly was done by the Wolf, and Renaud, after the shock of horor was past, gave a sigh of relief and added, "Eet is le Garou. He hab save my leel girl from zat Paul. He always was good to children."

6

This was the cause of the great final hunt that they fixed for Christmas Day just two years after the scene at the grave of Little Jim. It seemed as though all the Dogs in the country were brought together. The three Huskies were there—the Factor considered them essential—there were Danes and trailers and a rabble of farm Dogs and nondescripts. They spent the morning beating all the woods east of St. Boniface and had no success. But a telephone message came that the trail they sought had been seen near the Assiniboine woods west of the city, and an hour later the hunt was yelling on the hot scent of the Winnipeg Wolf.

Away they went, a rabble of Dogs, a motley rout of horsemen, a mob of men and boys on foot. Garou had no fear of the Dogs, but men he knew had guns and were dangerous. He led off for the dark timber-line of the Assiniboine, but the horsemen had open country and they headed him back. He coursed along the Colony Creek hollow and so eluded the bullets already flying. He made for a barb-wire fence, and passing that he got rid of the horsemen for a time, but still must keep the hollow that baffled the bullets. The Dogs were now closing on him. All he might have asked would probably have been to be left alone with them—forty or fifty to one as they were—he would have taken the odds. The Dogs were all around him now, but none dared to close in. A lanky Hound, trusting to his speed, ran alongside at length and got a side chop from Garou that laid him low. The horsemen were forced to take a distant way around, but now the chase was toward the town, and more men and Dogs came running out to join the fray.

The Wolf turned toward the slaughter-house, a familiar resort, and the shooting ceased on account of the houses, as well as the Dogs, being so near. These were indeed now close enough to encircle him and hinder all further flight. He looked for a place to guard his rear for a final stand, and seeing a wooden foot-bridge over a gutter he sprang in, there faced about and held the pack at bay. The men got bars and demolished the bridge. He leaped out, knowing now that he had to die, but ready, wishing only to make a worthy fight, and then for the first time in broad day view of all his foes he stood—the shadowy Dog-killer, the disembodied voice of St. Boniface woods, the wonderful Winnipeg Wolf.

7

At last after three long years of fight he stood before them alone, confronting twoscore Dogs, and men with guns to back them—but facing them just as resolutely as I saw him that day in the wintry woods. The same old curl was on his lips—the hard-knit flanks heaved just a little, but his green and yellow eye glowed steadily. The Dogs closed in, led not by the huge Huskies from the woods—they evidently knew too much for that—but by a Bulldog from the town; there was scuffling of many feet; a low rumbling for a time replaced the yapping of the pack; a flashing of those red and grizzled jaws, a momentary hurl back of the onset, and again he stood alone and braced, the grim and grand old bandit that he was. Three times they tried and suffered. Their boldest were lying about him. The first to go down was the Bulldog. Learning wisdom now, the Dogs held back, less sure; but his square-built chest showed never a sign of weakness yet, and after waiting impatiently he advanced a few steps, and thus, alas! gave to the gunners their long-expected chance. Three rifles rang, and in the snow Garou went down at last, his life of combat done.

He had made his choice. His days were short and crammed with quick events. His tale of many peaceful years was spent in three of daily brunt. He picked his trail, a new trail, high and short. He chose to drink his cup at a single gulp, and break the glass—but he left a deathless name

Who can look into the mind of the Wolf? Who can show us his wellspring of motive? Why should he still cling to a place of endless tribulation? It could not be because he knew no other country, for the region is limitless, food is everywhere, and he was known at least as far as Selkirk. Nor could his motive be revenge. No animal will give up its whole life to seeking revenge; that evil kind of mind is found in man alone. The brute creation seeks for peace.

There is then but one remaining bond to chain him, and that the strongest claim that anything can own—the mightiest force on earth.

The Wolf is gone. The last relic of him was lost in the burning Grammar School, but to this day the sexton of St. Boniface Church avers that the tolling bell on Christmas Eve never fails to provoke that weird and melancholy Wolf-cry from the wooded graveyard a hundred steps away, where they laid his Little Jim, the only being on earth that ever met him with the touch of love.

The White Reindeer

The White Reindeer

Skoal! Skoal! For Norway Skoal!
Sing ye the song of the Vand-dam troll.
    When I am hiding
     Norway's luck
     On a White Storbuk
Comes riding, riding.

THE SETTING

 LEAK, black, deep, and cold is Utrovand, a long pocket of glacial water, a crack in the globe, a wrinkle in the high Norwegian mountains, blocked with another mountain, and flooded with a frigid flood, three thousand feet above its Mother Sea, and yet no closer to its Father Sun. Around its cheerless shore is a belt of stunted trees, that sends a long tail up the high valley, till it dwindles away to sticks and moss, as it also does some half-way up the granite hills that rise a thousand feet, encompassing the lake. This is the limit of trees, the end of the growth of wood. The birch and willow are the last to drop out of the long fight with frost. Their miniature thickets are noisy with the cries of Fieldfare, Pipit, and Ptarmigan, but these are left behind on nearing the upper plateau, where shade of rock and sough of wind are all that take their place. The chilly Hoifjeld rolls away, a rugged, rocky plain, with great patches of snow in all the deeper hollows, and the distance blocked by snowy peaks that rise and roll and whiter gleam, till, dim and dazzling in the north, uplifts the Jötunheim, the home of spirits, of glaciers, and of the lasting snow.

The treeless stretch is one vast attest to the force of heat. Each failure of the sun by one degree is marked by a lower realm of life. The northern slope of each hollow is less boreal than its southern side. The pine and spruce have given out long ago; the mountain-ash went next; the birch and willow climbed up half the slope. Here, nothing grows but creeping plants and moss. The plain itself is pale grayish green, one vast expanse of reindeer-moss, but warmed at spots into orange by great beds of polytrichum, and, in sunnier nooks, deepened to a herbal green. The rocks that are scattered everywhere are of a delicate lilac, but each is variegated with spreading frill-edged plasters of gray-green lichen or orange powder-streaks and beauty-spots of black. These rocks have great power to hold the heat, so that each of them is surrounded by a little belt of heat-loving plants that could not otherwise live so high. Dwarfed representatives of the birch and willow both are here, hugging the genial rock, as an old French *habitant* hugs his stove in winter-time, spreading their branches over it, instead of in the frigid air. A foot away is seen a chillier belt of heath, and farther off, colder, where none else can grow, is the omnipresent gray-green reindeer-moss that gives its color to the upland. The hollows are still filled with snow, though now it is June. But each of these white expanses is shrinking, spending itself in ice-cold streams that somehow reach the lake. These *snö-fläcks* show no sign of life, not even the 'red-snow' tinge, and around each is a belt of barren earth, to testify that life and warmth can never be divorced.

Birdless and lifeless, the gray-green snow-pied waste extends over all the stretch that is here between the timber-line and the snow-line, above which winter never quits its hold. Farther north both come lower, till the timber-line is at the level of the sea; and all the land is in that treeless belt called Tundra in the Old World, and Barrens in the New, and that everywhere is the Home of the Reindeer—the Realm of the Reindeer-moss.

1

In and out it flew, in and out, over the water and under, as the Varsimlé, the leader doe of the Reindeer herd, walked past on the vernal banks, and it sang:—

"Skoal! Skoal! Gamle Norge Skoal!" and more about "a White Reindeer and Norway's good luck," as though the singer were gifted with special insight.

When old Sveggum built the Vand-dam on the Lower Hoif-jeld, just above the Utrovand, and set his *ribesten* a-going, he supposed that he was the owner of it all. But some one was there before him. And in and out of the spouting stream this some one dashed, and sang songs that he made up to fit the place and the time. He skipped from *skjæke* to *skjæke* of the wheel, and did many things which Sveggum could set down only to luck—whatever that is; and some said that Sveggum's luck was a Wheel-troll, a Water-fairy, with a brown coat and a white beard, one that lived on land or in water, as he pleased.

But most of Sveggum's neighbors saw only a Fossekal, the little Waterfall Bird that came each year and danced in the stream, or dived where the pool is deep. And maybe both were right, for some of the very oldest peasants will tell you that a Fairy-troll may take the form of a man or the form of a bird. Only this bird lived a life no bird can live, and sang songs that men never had sung in Norway. Wonderful vision had he, and sights he saw that man never saw. For the Fieldfare would build before him, and the Lemming fed its brood under his very eyes. Eyes were they to see; for the dark speck on Suletind that man could barely glimpse was a Reindeer, with half-shed coat, to him; and the green slime on the Vandren was beautiful green pasture with a banquet spread.

Oh, Man is so blind, and makes himself so hated! But Fossekal harmed none, so none were afraid of him. Only he sang, and his songs were sometimes mixed with fun and prophecy, or perhaps a little scorn.

From the top of the tassel-birch he could mark the course of the Vand-dam stream past the Nystuen hamlet to lose itself in the gloomy waters of Utrovand; or by a higher flight he could see across the barren upland that rolled to Jötunheim in the north.

The great awakening was on now. The springtime had already reached the woods; the valleys were a-throb with life; new birds coming from the south, winter sleepers reappearing, and the Reindeer that had wintered in the lower woods should soon again be seen on the uplands.

Not without a fight do the Frost Giants give up the place so long their own; a great battle was in progress; but the Sun was slowly, surely winning, and driving them back to their Jötunheim. At every hollow and shady place they made another stand, or sneaked back by night, only to suffer another defeat. Hard hitters these, as they are stubborn fighters; many a granite rock was split and shattered by their blows in reckless fight, so that its inner fleshy tints were shown and warmly gleamed among the gray-green rocks that dotted the plain, like the countless flocks of Thor. More or less of these may be found at every place of battle-brunt, and straggled along the slope of Suletind was a host that reached for half a mile. But stay! these moved. Not rocks were they, but living creatures.

They drifted along erratically, yet one way, all up the wind. They swept out of sight in a hollow, to reappear on a ridge much nearer, and serried there against the sky, we marked their branching horns, and knew them for the Reindeer in their home.

The band came drifting our way, feeding like Sheep, grunting like only themselves. Each one found a grazing-spot, stood there till it was cleared off, then trotted on crackling hoofs to the front in search of another. So the band was ever changing in rank and form. But one there was that was always at or near the van—a large and well-favored Simlé, or Hind. However much the band might change and spread, she was in the forefront, and the observant would soon have seen signs that she had an influence over the general movement—that she, indeed, was the leader. Even the big Bucks, in their huge velvet-clad antlers, admitted this untitular control; and if one, in a

spirit of independence, evinced a disposition to lead else-
where, he soon found himself uncomfortably alone.

The Varsimlé, or leading Hind, had kept the band hover-
ing, for the last week or two, along the timber-line, going
higher each day to the baring uplands, where the snow was
clearing and the deer-flies were blown away. As the pasture
zone had climbed she had followed in her daily foraging, returning to the sheltered woods at sundown, for the wild things
fear the cold night wind even as man does. But now the deer-
flies were rife in the woods, and the rocky hillside nooks warm
enough for the nightly bivouac, so the woodland was deserted.

Probably the leader of a band of animals does not consciously pride itself on leadership, yet has an uncomfortable
sensation when not followed. But there are times with all
when solitude is sought. The Varsimlé had been fat and well
through the winter, yet now was listless, and lingered with
drooping head as the grazing herd moved past her.

Sometimes she stood gazing blankly while the unchewed
bunch of moss hung from her mouth, then roused to go on
to the front as before; the spells of vacant stare and the hankering to be alone grew stronger. She turned downward to
seek the birch woods, but the whole band turned with her. She
stood stock-still, with head down. They grazed and grunted
past, leaving her like a statue against the hillside. When all
had gone on, she slunk quietly away; walked a few steps,
looked about, made a pretense of grazing, snuffed the ground,
looked after the herd, and scanned the hills; then downward
fared toward the sheltering woods.

Once as she peered over a bank she sighted another Simlé,
a doe Reindeer, uneasily wandering by itself. But the Varsimlé wished not for company. She did not know why, but she

felt that she must hide away somewhere.

She stood still until the other had passed on, then turned aside, and went with faster steps and less wavering, till she came in view of Utrovand, away down by the little stream that turns old Sveggum's ribesten. Up above the dam she waded across the limpid stream, for deep-laid and sure is the instinct of a wild animal to put running water between itself and those it shuns. Then, on the farther bank, now bare and slightly green, she turned, and passing in and out among the twisted trunks, she left the noisy Vand-dam. On the higher ground beyond she paused, looked this way and that, went on a little, but returned; and here, completely shut in by softly painted rocks, and birches wearing little springtime hangers, she seemed inclined to rest; yet not to rest, for she stood uneasily this way and that, driving away the flies that settled on her legs, heeding not at all the growing grass, and thinking she was hid from all the world.

But nothing escapes the Fossekal. He had seen her leave the herd, and now he sat on a gorgeous rock that overhung, and sang as though he had waited for this and knew that the fate of the nation might turn on what passed in this far glen. He sang:

> Skoal! Skoal! For Norway Skoal!
> Sing ye the song of the Vand-dam troll.
>   When I am hiding
>   Norway's luck
>   On a White Storbuk
>   Comes riding, riding.

There are no Storks in Norway, and yet an hour later there

was a wonderful little Reindeer lying beside the Varsimlé. She was brushing his coat, licking and mothering him, proud and happy as though this was the first little Renskalv ever born. There might be hundreds born in the herd that month, but probably no more like this one, for he was snowy white, and the song of the singer on the painted rock was about

> Good luck, good luck,
> And a White Storbuk,

as though he foresaw clearly the part that the White Calf was to play when he grew to be a Storbuk.

But another wonder now came to pass. Before an hour, there was a second little Calf—a brown one this time. Strange things happen, and hard things are done when they needs must. Two hours later, when the Varsimlé led the White Calf away from the place, there was no Brown Calf, only some flattened rags with calf-hair on them.

The mother was wise: better one strongling than two weaklings. Within a few days the Simlé once more led the band, and running by her side was the White Calf. The Varsimlé considered him in all things, so that he really set the pace for the band, which suited very well all the mothers that now had Calves with them. Big, strong, and wise was the Varsimlé, in the pride of her strength, and this White Calf was the flower of her prime. He often ran ahead of his mother as she led the herd, and Rol, coming on them one day, laughed aloud at the sight as they passed, old and young, fat Simlé and antlered Storbuk, a great brown herd, all led, as it seemed, by a little White Calf.

So they drifted away to the high mountains, to be gone all

summer. "Gone to be taught by the spirits who dwell where the Black Loon laughs on the ice," said Lief of the Lower Dale; but Sveggum, who had always been among the Reindeer, said: "Their mothers are the teachers, even as ours are."

When the autumn came, old Sveggum saw a moving snö-fläck far off on the brown moorland; but the Troll saw a white yearling, a Nekbuk; and when they ranged alongside of Utrovand to drink, the still sheet seemed fully to reflect the White One, though it barely sketched in the others, with the dark hills behind.

Many a little Calf had come that spring, and had drifted away on the moss-barrens, to come back no more; for some were weaklings and some were fools; some fell by the way, for that is law; and some would not learn the rules, and so died. But the White Calf was strongest of them all, and he was wise, so he learned of his mother, who was wisest of them all. He learned that the grass on the sun side of a rock is sweet, and though it looks the same in the dark hollows, it is there worthless. He learned that when his mother's hoofs crackled he must be up and moving, and when all the herd's hoofs crackled there was danger, and he must keep by his mother's side. For this crackling is like the whistling of a Whistler Duck's wings: it is to keep the kinds together. He learned that where the little Bomuldblomster hangs its cotton tufts is dangerous bog; that the harsh cackle of the Ptarmigan means that close at hand are Eagles, as dangerous for Fawn as for Bird. He learned that the little troll-berries are deadly, that when the *verra*-flies come stinging he must take refuge on a snow-patch, and that of all animals smells only that of his mother was to be fully trusted. He learned that he was growing. His flat calf sides and big joints were changing to the full barrel and clean limbs of the Yearling, and the little bumps which began to show on his head when he was only a fortnight old were now sharp, hard spikes that could win in a fight.

More than once they had smelt that dreaded destroyer of the north that men call the Gjerv or Wolverine; and one day, as this danger-scent came suddenly and in great strength, a huge blot of dark brown sprang rumbling from a rocky ledge, and straight for the foremost—the White Calf. His eye caught the flash of a whirling, shaggy mass, with gleaming teeth and eyes, hot-breathed and ferocious. Blank horror set his hair on end; his nostrils flared in fear: but before he fled there rose within another feeling—one of anger at the breaker of his peace, a sense that swept all fear away, braced his legs, and set his horns at charge. The brown brute landed with a deep-chested growl, to be received on the young one's spikes. They pierced him deeply, but the shock was overmuch; it bore the White One down, and he might yet have been killed but that his mother, alert and ever near, now charged the attacking monster, and heavier, better armed, she hurled and speared him to the ground. And the White Calf, with a very demon glare in his once mild eyes, charged too; and even after the Wolverine was a mere hairy mass, and his mother had retired to feed, he came, snorting out his rage, to drive his spikes into the hateful thing, till his snowy head was stained with his adversary's blood.

Thus he showed that below the ox-like calm exterior was the fighting beast; that he was like the men of the north, rugged, square-built, calm, slow to wrath, but when aroused "seeing red."

When they ranked together by the lake that fall, the Fossekal sang his old song:

When I am hiding
Norway's luck
On a White Storbuk
Comes riding, riding,

as though this was something he had awaited, then disappeared no one knew where. Old Sveggum had seen it flying through the stream, as birds fly through the air, walking in the bottom of a deep pond as a Ptarmigan walks on the rocks, living as no bird can live; and now the old man said it had simply gone southward for the winter. But old Sveggum could neither read nor write: how should he know?

2

Each springtime when the Reindeer passed over Sveggum's mill-run, as they moved from the lowland woods to the bleaker shore of Utrovand, the Fossekal was there to sing about the White Storbuk, which each year became more truly the leader.

That first spring he stood little higher than a Hare. When he came to drink in the autumn, his back was above the rock where Sveggum's stream enters Utrovand. Next year he barely passed under the stunted birch, and the third year the Fossekal on the painted rock was looking up, not down, at him as he passed. This was the autumn when Rol and Sveggum sought the Hoifjeld to round up their half-wild herd and select some of the strongest for the sled. There was but one opinion about the Storbuk. Higher than the others, heavier, white as snow, with a mane that swept the shallow drifts, breasted like a Horse and with horns like a storm-grown oak, he was king of the herd, and might easily be king of the road.

There are two kinds of deer-breakers, as there are two kinds of horse-breakers: one that tames and teaches the animal, and gets a spirited, friendly helper; one that aims to break its spirit, and gets only a sullen slave, ever ready to rebel and wreak its hate. Many a Lapp and many a Norsk has paid with his life for brutality to his Reindeer, and Rol's days were shortened by his own pulk-Ren. But Sveggum was of gentler sort. To him fell the training of the White Storbuk. It was slow, for the Buck resented all liberties from man, as he did from his brothers; but kindness, not fear, was the power that tamed him, and when he had learned to obey and glory in the sled race, it was a noble sight to see the great white mild-eyed beast striding down the long snow-stretch of Utrovand, the steam jetting from his nostrils, the snow swirling up before like the curling waves on a steamer's bow, sled, driver, and Deer all dim in flying white.

Then came the Yule-tide Fair, with the races on the ice, and Utrovand for once was gay. The sullen hills about re-echoed with merry shouting. The Reindeer races were first, with many a mad mischance for laughter. Rol himself was there with his swiftest sled Deer, a tall, dark, five-year-old, in his primest prime. But over-eager, over-brutal, he harried the sullen, splendid slave till in mid-race—just when in a way to win—it turned at a cruel blow, and Rol took refuge under the upturned sled until it had vented its rage against the wood; and so he lost the race, and the winner was the young White Storbuk. Then he won the five-mile race around the lake; and for each triumph Sveggum hung a little silver bell on his harness, so that now he ran and won to merry music.

Then came the Horse races,—running races these; the Reindeer only trots,—and when Balder, the victor Horse, received his ribbon and his owner the purse, came Sveggum with all his winnings, in his hand, and said: "Ho, Lars, thine is a fine Horse, but mine is a better Storbuk; let us put our winnings together and race, each his beast, for all."

A Ren against a Race-horse—such a race was never seen till now. Off at the pistol-crack they flew. "Ho, Balder! (*cluck!*) Ho, hi, Balder!" Away shot the beautiful Racer, and the Storbuk, striding at a slower trot, was left behind.

"Ho, Balder!" "Hi, Storbuk!" How the people cheered as the Horse went bounding and gaining! But he had left the line at his top speed; the Storbuk's rose as he flew—faster—faster. The Pony ceased to gain. A mile whirled by; the gap began to close. The Pony had over-spurted at the start, but the Storbuk was warming to his work—striding evenly, swiftly, faster yet, as Sveggum cried in encouragement: "Ho, Storbuk! good Storbuk!" or talked to him only with a gentle rein. At the turning-point the pair were neck and neck; then the Pony —though well driven and well shod—slipped on the ice, and thenceforth held back as though in fear, so the Storbuk steamed away. The Pony and his driver were far behind when a roar from every human throat in Filefjeld told that the Storbuk had passed the wire and won the race. And yet all this was before the White Ren had reached the years of his full strength and speed.

Once that day Rol essayed to drive the Storbuk. They set off at a good pace, the White Buk ready, responsive to the single rein, and his mild eyes veiled by his drooping lashes. But, without any reason other than the habit of brutality, Rol struck him. In a moment there was a change. The Racer's speed was checked, all four legs braced forward till he stood; the drooping lids were raised, the eyes rolled—there was a green light in them now. Three puffs of steam were jetted from each nostril. Rol shouted, then, scenting danger, quickly upset the sled and hid beneath. The Storbuk turned to charge the sled, sniffing and tossing the snow with his foot; but little Knute, Sveggum's son, ran forward and put his arms around the Storbuk's neck; then the fierce look left the Reindeer's eye, and he suffered the child to lead him quietly back to the starting-point. Beware, O driver! the Reindeer, too, "sees red."

This was the coming of the White Storbuk for the folk of Filefjeld.

In the two years that followed he became famous throughout that country as Sveggum's Storbuk, and many a strange exploit was told of him. In twenty minutes he could carry old Sveggum round the six miles rim of Utrovand. When the snow-slide buried all the village of Holaker, it was the Storbuk that brought the word for help to Opdalstole and returned again over the forty miles of deep snow in seven hours, to carry brandy, food, and promise of speedy aid.

When over-venturesome young Knute Sveggumsen broke through the new thin ice of Utrovand, his cry for help brought the Storbuk to the rescue; for he was the gentlest of his kind and always ready to come at call.

He brought the drowning boy in triumph to the shore, and as they crossed the Vand-dam stream, there was the Troll-bird to sing:

> Good luck, good luck,
> With the White Storbuk.

After which he disappeared for months—doubtless dived
into some subaqueous cave to feast and revel all winter; although Sveggum did not believe it was so.

3

How often is the fate of kingdoms given into child hands,
or even committed to the care of Bird or Beast! A She-wolf
nursed the Roman Empire. A Wren pecking crumbs on a
drum-head aroused the Orange army, it is said, and ended the
Stuart reign in Britain. Little wonder, then, that to a noble
Reindeer Buk should be committed the fate of Norway: that
the Troll on the wheel should have reason in his rhyme.

These were troublous times in Scandinavia. Evil men, trai-
tors at heart, were sowing dissension between the brothers
Norway and Sweden. "Down with the Union!" was becoming
the popular cry.

Oh, unwise peoples! If only you could have been by Sveggum's wheel to hear the Troll when he sang:

> The Raven and the Lion
>   They held the Bear at bay;
> But he picked the bones of both
>   When they quarrelled by the way.

Threats of civil war, of a fight for independence, were heard
throughout Norway. Meetings were held more or less secretly,
and at each of them was some one with well-filled pockets and
glib tongue, to enlarge on the country's wrongs, and promise
assistance from an outside irresistible power as soon as they

showed that they meant to strike for freedom. No one openly
named the power. That was not necessary; it was everywhere
felt and understood. Men who were real patriots began to believe in it. Their country was wronged. Here was one to set
her right. Men whose honor was beyond question became
secret agents of this power. The state was honey-combed and
mined; society was a tangle of plots. The king was helpless,
though his only wish was for the people's welfare. Honest and
straightforward, what could he do against this far-reaching
machination? The very advisers by his side were corrupted
through mistaken patriotism. The idea that they were playing into the hands of the foreigner certainly never entered
into the minds of these dupes—at least, not those of the rank
and file. One or two, tried, selected, and bought by the arch-
enemy, knew the real object in view, and the chief of these was
Borgrevinck, a former landsman of Nordlands. A man of unusual gifts, a member of the Storthing, a born leader, he might
have been prime minister long ago, but for the distrust in-
spired by several unprincipled dealings. Soured by what he
considered want of appreciation, balked in his ambition, he
was a ready tool when the foreign agent sounded him. At first
his patriotism had to be sopped, but that necessity disappeared
as the game went on, and perhaps he alone, of the whole far-
reaching conspiracy, was prepared to strike at the Union for
the benefit of the foreigner.

Plans were being perfected—army officers being secretly
misled and won over by the specious talk of "their country's
wrongs," and each move made Borgrevinck more surely the
head of it all—when a quarrel between himself and the "de-
liverer" occurred over the question of recompense. Wealth
untold they were willing to furnish; but regal power, never.

The quarrel became more acute. Borgrevinck continued to attend all meetings, but was ever more careful to center all power in himself, and even prepared to turn round to the king's party if necessary to further his ambition. The betrayal of his followers would purchase his own safety. But proofs he must have, and he set about getting signatures to a declaration of rights which was simply a veiled confession of treason. Many of the leaders he had deluded into signing this before the meeting at Laersdalsoren. Here they met in the early winter, some twenty of the patriots, some of them men of position, all of them men of brain and power. Here, in the close and stifling parlor, they planned, discussed, and questioned. Great hopes were expressed, great deeds were forecast, in that stove-hot room.

Outside, against the fence, in the winter night, was the Great White Reindeer, harnessed to a sled, but lying down with his head doubled back on his side as he slept, calm, unthoughtful, ox-like. Which seemed likelier to decide the nation's fate, the earnest thinkers indoors, or the ox-like sleeper without? Which seemed more vital to Israel, the bearded council in King Saul's tent, or the light-hearted shepherd-boy hurling stones across the brook at Bethlehem? At Laersdalsoren it was as before: deluded by Borgrevinck's eloquent plausibility, all put their heads in the noose, their lives and country in his hands, seeing in this treacherous monster a very angel of self-sacrificing patriotism. All? No, not all. Old Sveggum was there. He could neither read nor write. That was his excuse for not signing. He could not read a letter in a book, but he could read something of the hearts of men. As the meeting broke up he whispered to Axel Tanberg: "Is his own name on that paper?" And Axel,

starting at the thought, said: "No." Then said Sveggum: "I
don't trust that man. They ought to know of this at Nystuen."
For there was to be the really important meeting. But how
to let them know was the riddle. Borgrevinck was going there
at once with his fast Horses.

Sveggum's eye twinkled as he nodded toward the Storbuk,
standing tied to the fence. Borgrevinck leaped into his sleigh
and went off at speed, for he was a man of energy.

Sveggum took the bells from the harness, untied the Reindeer, stepped into the pulk. He swung the single rein, clucked
to the Storbuk, and also turned his head toward Nystuen.
The fast Horses had a long start, but before they had climbed
the eastward hill Sveggum needs must slack, so as not to over-
take them. He held back till they came to the turn above the
woods at Maristuen; then he quit the road, and up the river
flat he sped the Buk, a farther way, but the only way to bring
them there ahead.

Squeak, crack—squeak, crack—squeak, crack—at regular
intervals from the great spreading snow-shoes of the Storbuk,
and the steady sough of his breath was like the *Nordland*
as she passes up the Hardanger Fjord. High up, on the smooth
road to the left, they could hear the jingle of the horse-bells
and the shouting of Borgrevinck's driver, who, under orders,
was speeding hard for Nystuen.

The highway was a short road and smooth, and the river
valley was long and rough; but when, in four hours, Borgrevinck got to Nystuen, there in the throng was a face that he
had just left at Laersdalsoren. He appeared not to notice,
though nothing ever escaped him.

At Nystuen none of the men would sign. Some one had
warned them. This was serious; might be fatal at such a crit-
ical point. As he thought it over, his suspicions turned more

and more to Sveggum, the old fool that could not write his name at Laersdalsoren. But how did he get there before himself with his speedy Horses?

There was a dance at Nystuen that night; the dance was necessary to mask the meeting; and during that Borgrevinck learned of the swift White Ren.

The Nystuen trip had failed, thanks to the speed of the White Buk. Borgrevinck must get to Bergen before word of this, or all would be lost. There was only one way, to be sure of getting there before any one else. Possibly word had already gone from Laersdalsoren. But even at that, Borgrevinck could get there and save himself, at the price of all Norway, if need be, provided he went with the White Storbuk. He would not be denied. He was not the man to give up a point, though it took all the influence he could bring to bear, this time, to get old Sveggum's leave.

The Storbuk was quietly sleeping in the corner when Sveggum came to bring him. He rose leisurely, hind legs first, stretched one, then the other, curling his tail tight on his back as he did so, shook the hay from the great antlers as though they were a bunch of twigs, and slowly followed Sveggum at the end of the tight halter. He was so sleepy and slow that Borgrevinck impatiently gave him a kick, and got for response a short snort from the Buk, and from Sveggum an earnest warning, both of which were somewhat scornfully received. The tinkling bells on the harness had been replaced, but Borgrevinck wanted them removed. He wished to go in silence. Sveggum would not be left behind when his favorite Ren went forth, so he was given a seat in the horse-sleigh which was to follow, and the driver thereof received from his master a secret hint to delay.

Then, with papers on his person to death-doom a multitude

of misguided men, with fiendish intentions in his heart as well as the power to carry them out, and with the fate of Norway in his hands, Borgrevinck was made secure in the sled, behind the White Storbuk, and sped at dawn on his errand of desolation.

At the word from Sveggum the White Ren set off with a couple of bounds that threw Borgrevinck back in the pulk. This angered him, but he swallowed his wrath on seeing that it left the horse-sleigh behind. He shook the line, shouted, and the Buk settled down to a long, swinging trot. His broad hoofs clicked double at every stride. His nostrils, out level, puffed steady blasts of steam in the frosty morning as he settled to his pace. The pulk's prow cut two long shears of snow, that swirled up over man and sled till all were white. And the great ox-eyes of the King Ren blazed joyously in the delight of motion, and of conquest too, as the sound of the horse-bells faded far behind.

Even masterful Borgrevinck could not but mark with pleasure the noble creature that had balked him last night and now was lending its speed to his purpose; for it was his intention to arrive hours before the horse-sleigh, if possible.

Up the rising road they sped as though downhill, and the driver's spirits rose with the exhilarating speed. The snow groaned ceaselessly under the prow of the pulk, and the frosty creaking under the hoofs of the flying Ren was like the gritting of mighty teeth. Then came the level stretch from Nystuen's hill to Dalecarl's, and as they whirled by in the early day, little Carl chanced to peep from a window, and got sight of the Great White Ren in a white pulk with a white driver, just as it is in the stories of the Giants, and clapped his hands, and cried, "Good, good!"

But his grandfather, when *he* caught a glimpse of the white wonder that went without even sound of bells, felt a cold chill in his scalp, and went back to light a candle that he kept at the window till the sun was high, for surely this was the Storbuk of Jötunheim.

But the Ren whirled on, and the driver shook the reins and thought only of Bergen. He struck the White Steed with the loose end of the rope. The Buk gave three great snorts and three great bounds, then faster went, and as they passed by Dyrskaur, where the Giant sits on the edge, his head was muffled in scud, which means that a storm is coming. The Storbuk knew it. He sniffed, and eyed the sky with anxious look, and even slacked a little; but Borgrevinck yelled at the speeding beast, though going yet as none but he could go, and struck him once, twice, and thrice, and harder yet. So the pulk was whirled along like a skiff in a steamer's wake; but there was blood in the Storbuk's eye now; and Borgrevinck was hard put to balance the sled. The miles flashed by like roods till Sveggum's bridge appeared. The storm-wind now was blowing, but there was the Troll. Whence came he now, none knew, but there he was, hopping on the keystone and singing of

> Norway's fate and Norway's luck,
> Of the hiding Troll and the riding Buk.

Down the winding highway they came, curving inward as they swung around the corner. At the voice on the bridge the Deer threw back his ears and slackened his pace. Borgrevinck, not knowing whence it came, struck savagely at the Ren. The red light gleamed in those ox-like eyes. He snorted

in anger and shook the great horns, but he did not stop to
avenge the blow. For him was a vaster vengeance still. He
onward sped as before, but from that time Borgrevinck had
lost all control. The one voice that the Ren would hear had
been left behind. They whirled aside, off the road, before
the bridge was reached. The pulk turned over, but righted
itself, and Bargrevinck would have been thrown out and killed
but for the straps. It was not to be so; it seemed rather as
though the every curse of Norway had been gathered into
the sled for a purpose. Bruised and battered, he reappeared.
The Troll from the bridge leaped lightly to the Storbuk's
head, and held on to the horns as he danced and sang his
ancient song, and a new song, too:

> Ha! at last! Oh, lucky day,
> Norway's curse to wipe away!

Borgrevinck was terrified and furious. He struck harder at
the Storbuk as he bounded over the rougher snow, and vainly
tried to control him. He lost his head in fear. He got out
his knife, at last, to strike at the wild Buk's hamstrings, but
a blow from the hoof sent it flying from his hand. Their
speed on the road was slow to that they now made: no longer
striding at the trot, but bounding madly, great five-stride
bounds, the wretched Borgrevinck strapped in the sled, alone
and helpless through his own contriving, screaming, cursing,
and praying. The Storbuk with bloodshot eyes, madly steaming, careered up the rugged ascent, up to the broken, stormy
Hoifjeld; mounting the hills as a Petrel mounts the rollers,
skimming the flat as a Fulmar skims the shore, he followed
the trail where his mother had first led his tottering steps,

up from the Vand-dam nook. He followed the old familiar
route that he had followed for five years, where the white-
winged Rype flies aside, where the black rock mountains, shining white, come near and block the sky, "where the Reindeer
find their mysterie."

On like the little snow-wreath that the storm-wind sends
dancing before the storm, on like a whirlwind over the
shoulder of Suletind, over the knees of Torholmenbræ—
the Giants that sit at the gateway. Faster than man or beast
could follow, up—up—up—and on; and no one saw them
go, but a Raven that swooped behind, and flew as Raven
never flew, and the Troll, the same old Troll that sang by
the Vand-dam, and now danced and sang between the antlers:

> Good luck, good luck for Norway
> With the White Storbuk comes riding.

Over Tvindehoug they faded like flying scud on the moor-
lands, on to the gloomy distance, away toward Jötunheim,
the home of the Evil spirits, the Land of the Last Snow. Their
every sign and trail was wiped away by the drifting storm,
and the end of them no man knows.

The Norse folk awoke as from a horrid nightmare. Their
national ruin was averted; there were no deaths, for there
were no proofs; and the talebearer's strife was ended.

The one earthly sign remaining from that drive is the string
of silver bells that Sveggum had taken from the Storbuk's
neck—the victory bells, each the record of a triumph won;
and when the old man came to understand, he sighed, and
hung to the string a final bell, the largest of them all.

Nothing more was ever seen or heard of the creature who

so nearly sold his country, or of the White Storbuk who balked him. Yet those who live near Jötunheim say that on stormy nights, when the snow is flying and the wind is raving in the woods, there sometimes passes, at frightful speed, an enormous White Reindeer with fiery eyes, drawing a snow-white pulk, in which is a screaming wretch in white, and on the head of the Deer, balancing by the horns, is a brown-clad, white-bearded Troll, bowing and grinning pleasantly at him, and singing

> Of Norway's luck
> And a White Storbuk—

the same, they say, as the one that with prophetic vision sang by Sveggum's Vand-dam on a bygone day when the birches wore their springtime hangers, and a great mild-eyed Varsimlé came alone, to go away with a little white Renskalv walking slowly, demurely, by her side.